Bug Out! California

Creeping Tyranny

Robert Boren

South Bay Press

Author/Publishing South Bay Press

Publisher's Note: This is a work of fiction. Names, characters, places, and incidents are a product of the author's imagination. Locales and public names are sometimes used for atmospheric purposes. Any resemblance to actual people, living or dead, or to businesses, companies, events, institutions, or locales is completely coincidental.

Book Layout ©2017 BookDesignTemplates.com
Bug Out! California: Creeping Tyranny/ Robert Boren. -- 1st ed.
ISBN 9781973335191

For Laura

You have enemies? Good. That means you've stood up for something, sometime in your life.

—Winston Churchill

Contents

Dulzura Full-Timers

T he sleepy RV Park was finally cooling down, a light breeze coming from the west.

"You coming, Sarah?" John asked, standing by the doorway of the motor home.

"I don't want to go," said Sarah, a woman in her early 60s. She walked out of the bedroom. "Can't you go by yourself?"

"I hate going alone," he said, watching her, disappointment in his eyes. He was nearly seventy, still a tall, strong man, but the deep lines in his face showed the pain of a long hard life.

"Why? What's the problem?" She sat in the dinette with a glass of water. John studied her, still attractive for her age with her rusty hair and trim figure.

"Half the time my friends don't show up, and then I sit there like a bump on a log."

"You should make new friends anyway," Sarah said. "You don't need me there for protection."

"Why don't you want to go?"

"You'll get drunk if your friends show up, and then I'll have to listen to you get sloppy," she said. "You know how I hate that."

"I don't get drunk that often," he said sharply.

"No, you don't, but you almost always do at these damn park barbecues," she said.

"What if I promise not to?"

She sighed and got up. "I'll tell you what. I'll go with you, and if your friends don't show up I'll stick around. We'll try to meet some new people there."

"There's a *but* coming," John said.

"If your friends are there, I'll come up with an excuse to leave early," she said. "Deal?"

John shook his head. "I guess that's the best I'll get. Deal."

"Good, then I'll go get dressed." She walked into the bedroom again. John looked out the front windshield. The Dulzura RV Park was nearly full. Unusual. Most of the people at the RV Park were retirees who lived there full time, enjoying the rural area just north of the Mexican border. There were always a few coaches passing through, but it was rare that all twenty of the non-residential sites were full. *Maybe there's a festival going on nearby.* He pulled down the shades in front of the windshield and plopped into the recliner by the door.

Sarah came out, dressed in an attractive blouse and pants. "Ready?"

John got up. "You look lovely."

"Thanks." She smiled. "You don't look so bad yourself."

"Yeah, for an old guy," he said as he opened the door. He waited for Sarah to walk down the steps and closed the door behind him. They walked through the tight rows of coaches towards the clubhouse, the smell of barbecue drifting towards them.

"My, there are so many people here," Sarah said, looking around.

"I know," John said. "Noticed that when I was looking out the windshield earlier. Is there a festival this weekend?"

"Not that I've heard," she said. They entered the clubhouse. Several of John's friends were sitting in the back, having an intense discussion as they watched the TV screen next to the stage.

"Looks like Clem, Harry, and Sid are here," John said, almost sounding disappointed. "Can I make a new deal?"

She shrugged. "Let's have it."

"Will you stick around if I don't drink?"

"You won't drink at all? No beers? No shots?"

"I promise. I'll drink coke instead."

She looked him in the eye for a long moment, then sighed. "Okay, deal."

They walked to the cooler. John reached in for a can of coke. "Want one?"

"Sure," Sarah said. They took their wet, icy cans and sat at the table.

"John and Sarah," said the grinning old man sitting in the center of the bench. "Glad you could make it."

"Thanks, Clem," John said.

"Not drinking, eh?" he asked, grinning wider, a few teeth missing. His scraggly white hair made him look even older than his 75 years.

"Thought I'd lay off tonight," John said.

"Sarah, you're looking lovely, as usual," Sid said, his longish jet-black hair partially covering a wrinkled face.

"He's had too much fire water," Harry cracked. He was a heavy-set bald man in his late sixties with a mischievous smile.

"That's racist," Sid said with half a frown. Everybody at the table laughed.

"Where are your wives?" Sarah asked.

"Oh, they'll be back," Harry said. "Our conversation was scaring them a little, I think."

"What conversation?" Sarah asked.

"We were talking to a couple from San Diego this morning," Sid said. "Hank and Linda. They were spewing all kinds of BS."

"What kind of BS?" John asked.

"They told us we should pull up stakes and vamoose," Sid said. "Said things were gonna get crazy in California, and we'd be nuts to stay."

"Where are they?" Sarah asked. "They gonna be here?"

"No, they were just overnighting. Left already, headed for Quartzsite."

"So what'd they say?" John asked.

"They were living in one of those high-rise condos on Mission Bay," Harry said. "Things were happening there all of a sudden."

"What kinds of things?" Sarah asked. "Do I have to pull every sentence out of you guys? I won't get scared."

Harry and Clem looked at each other. Sid shook his head, looking tired of the conversation.

"Lots of people coming over the border," Harry said. "Hank said they looked different. He said they looked like soldiers, not the usual peasants."

"He said the *usual wetbacks*," Sid said. "That guy was a jerk."

"I was trying not to repeat that," Harry said. "Anyway, he also said he heard some of them speaking Arabic."

John laughed. "Oh, please. One of those, eh?"

"That's what I thought at first," Clem said. "There was something really strange about those two."

"What do you mean?" Sarah asked.

"Linda, the wife," Clem said. "She looked totally shell-shocked. Right on the verge of a breakdown. She finally went into their coach to get away from the conversation."

"Maybe she was sick of her husband's BS," John said.

"That's not the vibe I got," Clem said, a grim look on his face. "She clung to him as if he was her only protector during most of the conversation. Only left when she got too scared. There was no contempt or embarrassment there. She looked like she worshiped this guy, and believed everything he was saying."

"I thought she looked depressed, or maybe tipping into dementia," Harry said. "Hank acted over-protective too, as one would act with a spouse that was sick."

"What was the gist of this guy's story?" John asked.

"Basically, that there's an invasion coming, and that people better get away from the border," Sid said. "Sounded like a story from one of those survivalist web sites."

Two women walked over, both in their mid-sixties. One had silver hair and a little too much makeup, smartly dressed. The other had dark hair, braided, with a younger look to her. Sid stood up and took the hand of the dark-haired woman.

"Yvonne," he said, pulling her next to him.

"Are you guys done with that stupid conversation?" She sat next to him.

"Just about," he said. "We were filling in John and Sarah."

"Oh," Yvonne said. "Hi, guys."

"Hi," Sarah said. John nodded.

The other woman sat next to Harry, settling close to him.

"Hey, honey," Harry said. "Glad you're back."

"You sure you're done talking about that idiot?" she asked. He nodded.

"Hi, Nancy," Sarah said.

"John's not drinking tonight?" she asked.

"Nope," Sarah said.

"Good," Nancy said. John shot her a glance, a thin smile on his face. He put his hand on Sarah's thigh and kissed her on the cheek.

"You guys see all the extra coaches?" John asked.

"Yeah, kinda weird," Yvonne said. "Wonder what's going on?"

"We were wondering the same thing," Sarah said.

"Maybe a new festival?" Nancy asked. "If so I'd like to go, depending on what it is. This place is a tad too isolated."

"I thought you loved living here," Harry said.

"Oh, I do, sweetie, but it's still nice to hit the town every once in a while," she said.

"Hey, look at the TV screen!" Sid said, pointing.

"My God, is that an airliner?" Clem asked. Video of a burning plane lying on the end of a runway showed on the screen, fire fighters hitting it with foam.

"Turn that up," Sarah said. John grabbed the remote off the corner of the stage and turned up the volume.

"The FAA has not confirmed that this plane was shot down as it was attempting takeoff, but eyewitness accounts say a rocket flashed up and hit its left wing, bringing the plane to the ground, where it exploded into flames. The FAA has confirmed that nobody survived the incident."

"What airport is that?" Yvonne asked.

"Look at the banner under the video," Sid said. "Lindbergh Field, San Diego."

***

Robbie Johnson sat at his laptop while the microwave zapped dinner, his large, trim frame hunched over too far to be comfortable, longish sable brown hair hanging over both sides of his face. He was angrily typing a message on yet another conspiracy message board, missing letters and slamming the backspace key to fix them on the fly. It was getting too dark. He reached over and switched on his desk lamp. There was a loud knock on the door.

"Dammit," he said, getting up and rushing to the window. His friend Gil was standing next to the door with a Winchester 30-30 rifle in his hands, looking around nervously. Robbie opened the door and he slipped in quickly.

"Are you nuts?" Robbie asked him. "You can't carry rifles around, man. The cops will lock you up."

"What cops?" Gil said, setting the rifle down next to the door. He dropped onto the couch, wiping sweat off his forehead and pushing his black hair back on his head. "Cops are afraid now, man. They're staying out of the way."

"Well then, one of those gang-bangers is gonna take that rifle away from you and shove it up your ass," Robbie told him. The microwave dinged. "There's my dinner."

"Go ahead," he said. "Don't mind me. I already ate."

"I wasn't going to," Robbie said as he walked into the kitchen of the tiny studio apartment.

"Got any beer?"

"Yeah, help yourself," Robbie said. "But only one or two. I don't want you firing that damn lever gun off in here."

"I wouldn't do that," Gil said, getting up. "Heard from Justin?"

"Yeah, he's coming over when he gets off work," Robbie said as he grabbed his meal out of the microwave. "Hand me one of those brews."

Gil nodded and passed him a beer, then opened his. He glanced at the screen of the laptop. "You messing with the nutcases again?"

Robbie laughed. "People got some strange-ass ideas out there."

There was the pop of gunfire in the distance.

"Dammit," Gil said. "It's getting closer. Gardena got real bad last night, dude. So did Carson."

"North Torrance isn't Gardena," Robbie said.

"Maybe we should split for a while," Gil said.

"Some of us have jobs. You know; we earn money at them."

"Shut up," Gil said. "I'll be back to work pretty soon."

"You don't seem to be in much of a hurry," Robbie said. There was a knock on the door. "That's probably Justin."

"I'll go check it out," Gil said, walking to the window. He glanced out and then opened the door.

"Hey, Justin," Robbie said.

"Hey, guys," he said. Justin was a tall skinny blonde with a crooked smile and muscular arms. He had a paper bag in his hands.

"What's that?" Gil asked.

"Chips, salsa, and beer," he said. "Breakfast of champions."

"Oh, brother," Robbie said.

"Crap, what's Gil's pea-shooter doing over here?" Justin asked.

"I didn't feel safe," Gil said. "So sue me."

"If the cops see you with that they'll run you in," Justin said, taking the bag to the kitchen counter. He emptied the contents, putting the beers in the fridge with the salsa. "Mind if I have one of yours while these get cold?"

"Help yourself," Robbie said.

There was the sound of a window breaking outside, and a woman screamed.

"Uh oh," Gil said, walking towards his gun. "*That* wasn't in Gardena."

"No, it wasn't," Robbie said, rushing to the back window. "I can't see that far down."

Shouting drifted up towards them, and another scream. More breaking glass.

"We should clear out of here," Gil said.

Robbie looked at him, then over at Justin. "And where do you suggest we go?"

"West," Gil said. "The trouble is all east and north."

There was a frantic knock at the door. "Guys, let me in."

"That's Steve," Robbie said. "Open the door."

Gill opened it and a red-haired young man rushed in, bowie knife in his hand.

"You okay?" Robbie asked as he watched him slam the door and put the night lock on.

"No," he said. "I got chased down the street, and now there's some gang-bangers messing with my car. If I didn't have my knife under the seat, I'd probably be toast."

"What are you doing here, anyway?" Robbie asked. "I thought you were working tonight."

"They shut down," Steve said, trying to catch his breath. "We can't stay here. There's a frigging mob on its way into the neighborhood. We better leave now."

"Told you, man," Justin said. "That lever gun loaded?"

"Hell yeah," Gil said. "Seven rounds. Got more in my pocket."

There was a crash outside, and the whoosh of a fire starting. "What the hell was that?" Steve asked.

Robbie looked out the back window again. "Somebody torched a car, I suspect. That's a big flame. Lighting the whole sky down there."

"Let's go to your folks house," Gil said. "They might be far enough west."

"North Redondo," Robbie said. "Maybe. I'll call them." He punched their land line into his cellphone and put it to his ear. After waiting a few moments, he spoke. "Mom, Dad, this is Robbie. We have to leave our apartment. It's getting bad here. We're coming over there. Call me."

"Not home?" Gil asked.

"Well, not answering anyway. I'll try my dad's cellphone." He hit the contact and waited a few moments, then ended the call and put the phone in his pocket. "No answer. Let's go. Want to take my car?"

"I'm not leaving mine here," Gil said.

"Me neither," Justin said.

"I don't want to leave mine," Steve said, "but those gang bangers were surrounding it, and its way down the street. Can I ride with you, man?"

Robbie nodded yes. "Let's take the beer and the food with us." He shut down his laptop, and then grabbed some grocery bags from the pantry and loaded the food and beer.

"Good idea," Justin said. He helped.

"Where's your car?" Gil asked. "In the garage?"

"Yeah," Robbie said. "Where's yours?"

"In the guest spot," Gil said.

"Mine's right in front of your building," Justin said.

Robbie put his laptop into the case. "Grab one of the food bags, Steve. The rest of you go downstairs. I'll meet you there. You all know how to get to my folk's house, right?"

"Yeah, it's off Artesia," Gil said.

"I remember," Justin said.

"Let's try to stay together," Robbie said. "Just pull into the driveway after me."

"Okay, man," Gil said. He picked up his rifle and opened the door, peering out. "Coast is clear."

"Good," Robbie said, picking up the laptop case. Steve picked up the bags of food, and they all slipped out the door. Robbie stopped to lock it up, and then they rushed along the second story walkway and down to the driveway and the garages below, shadowy in the dim light of the street lamps.

"I'll keep watch while you pull out," Gil said, his rifle at the ready. He stood just out of sight of the street, at the front edge of the building.

"Yeah, I'll keep watch too," Justin said, watching as the garage door opened.

Robbie and Steve threw the bags and the laptop into the trunk and got into the car. They backed out and headed down the driveway.

"Oh, crap," Steve said. Gil was in the middle of the driveway, aiming the rifle down Yukon Street to the left. Robbie pulled out far enough to see a mob of about twenty young men standing, watching Gil.

"Better stop, ese," one of the gang members shouted, moving forward.

"Get back, dude," Gil said. "I mean it."

"Let's get him," another of the gang said. "He won't really shoot. Look at him shaking."

Gil pulled the trigger, aiming a little high, the blast from the 30-30 echoing between the apartment buildings. The gang members ran away.

"C'mon, let's go before they come back," Justin shouted.

"Hey, they left my car," Steve said. "I'm gonna go get it."

"Okay, but hurry," Robbie said. "I'll wait until you get it started, just in case." Steve sprinted left down Yukon to his car and got in. He started it and drove up to Robbie's building.

"Let's go!" Robbie said. He turned right onto Yukon and punched it.

Gil nodded and jumped into his car, turning right onto the street. Justin followed, then Steve.

Robbie turned right on 168th Street, then left on Ainsworth, taking that to Artesia. Gunfire erupted to the east as he waited at the stop sign to turn west. He could see fires burning along Artesia to the east. Westbound traffic was heavy. He took the right turn, the others following him through, just in front of another clump of cars. They went under the 405 Freeway and crossed Prairie. There were crowds of people ahead, surrounding the intersection at Hawthorne Blvd.

Robbie's phone rang. He answered it.

"Yeah, Steve?"

"Just got a text from my sister. She said to stay away from the Galleria."

"I see, bunch of people flooding onto Hawthorne from the parking lot. Follow me. We'll make a U-turn and take Prairie to 190th Street."

"Got it," Steve said.

He set his phone down and made the U-turn, then made a right on Prairie and gunned it. He passed 182nd and was nearing 190th when he saw another gang, hanging out in the big park to the left. One of the gang members pointed at them, and then rocks and bottles flew. *Don't stop.* He made a fast right turn against the light, oncoming traffic honking as he floored his small Honda. He checked the rear-view mirror and saw his friends getting through their turn. They raced west until they were stopped at the big intersection with Hawthorne.

Robbie's phone rang again.

"Yeah, Steve?"

"Some jerk broke my passenger side window back there," he said, sounding out of breath. "We aren't gonna turn right on Inglewood Avenue, are we?"

"No, let's go all the way to Rindge," Robbie said. "Inglewood's too close to the Galleria."

"Good," he said. "Think your folk's place is far enough away?"

"No," Robbie said. "But any port in the storm tonight. It's defendable."

The light changed. Robbie ended the call and drove forward, feeling better as soon as he got across.

They made all the lights on the way down to Rindge Lane and turned right, entering dense middle-class housing with its one-way streets, numerous stop signs, and tight parking. It was quiet and peaceful in there, but nobody had their porch lights on. It took several minutes to get through all the stop signs to Grant Avenue. They waited for the light, then drove across, making a right turn on the second one-way street and following it down through more stop signs. The condo was several blocks down on the right. Robbie turned into the long driveway, going past the garage doors of the front and middle units. He stopped. His friends pulled in behind him, Steve hanging slightly into the street.

"I'm gonna check to see if they're home," Robbie said. "If they aren't, I'll pull this in the garage, and you guys can pull-in far enough to be out of the way of the other garages."

"Sound's good," Gil said.

"Hurry, my ass is hanging out," Steve said.

Robbie nodded, unlocked the front door, and went inside. It was quiet. Lucy, his parent's Jack Russell Terrier wasn't there. Neither was Mr. Wonderful the cat. He raced down the hall to the garage door and unlocked the bolt. The Jeep was missing. The garage door rolled up after he pressed the button on the door jamb. When it was up far enough he got into his Honda and drove it inside. The others pulled forward, taking the guest parking spot and the driveway past the middle unit's garage.

"They're out of town," Robbie said as he switched on the porch light.

"Hey, stagger the cars in the driveway so people can't run in here," Steve said.

"Good idea," Robbie said. Steve and Gil adjusted their cars. Justin pulled his car up further in the guest parking space to prevent somebody from opening the gate into the tiny backyard. They met inside the garage.

"How do you know they're out of town?" Gil asked.

"The dog and the cat are both gone," he said. "They've probably gone to the motor home. They took the Jeep Liberty. And look at the back door there."

Steve walked to the back of the garage as Robbie closed the main door. "Holy crap. Nobody's coming through there. Not even with one of those cop battering rams." He pointed to the four-by-four wedged between the work bench and the door.

"Simple but effective," Gil said, laughing.

"I'll help you with your stuff," Justin said.

"Me too," Steve said. Robbie nodded and opened the trunk. They picked up the bags and the laptop and left the garage, going down the hallway to the stairs by the front door. Robbie hit the lights and they walked up into the living area.

"We might not want to hang out here too long," Gil said, clutching his rifle as he looked out the sliding glass door to the balcony. "Your folks split for a reason, dude."

"Yeah, probably," Robbie said, staring up at the wall. "That's new." He pointed to a video camera.

"There was one in the garage, too," Steve said. "And outside, pointing at the front door."

Robbie laughed. "Didn't even notice. Let's get the food and beer in the fridge, and check things out. I'll bet I can access those cameras from my dad's PC."

{ 2 }

The Range

The south Torrance street curved towards Pacific Coast Highway, residents just now getting up as the sun came up.

"Trevor, you ready yet?" Seth asked. "It's a long drive." He was standing next to his late-model Toyota Four-Runner. Seth was just twenty-one, dark brown hair and eyebrows, medium build. He had an innocent look, with a clean complexion and a delicate mouth and nose, finished off by striking steel-gray eyes.

"Don't get your panties in a bunch," Trevor said, rushing out to the Four-Runner with his rifle case and a metal ammo box. "We got plenty of time." He opened the rear gate and placed his rifle next to Seth's, then shut it and went to the passenger side door, slipping his stout frame inside. Trevor was a redhead with freckles and mealy features. He wasn't handsome like Seth, but he made up for it with a witty and forceful personality and an athletic build. "Who else is going?"

"Angel and Matt," Seth said. "Maybe Matt's younger brother." He pulled away from the curve, driving down the tree-lined south Torrance street.

"I'm anxious to try out the new lever-guns," Trevor said as they pulled away.

"You sure they'll let us on the combat range this time?"

"Yeah, already made reservations. These guns are okay since they shoot pistol rounds," Trevor said. "They didn't want us to beat the hell out of their targets with 30-30 rounds when we asked before."

"I think that's a load of crap. They used to allow .223s on there, before the idiots in Sacramento passed the assault weapons ban."

"Well, a 30-30 carries a lot more punch in short range than a .223," Trevor said. "It's all about the weight of the bullet for short range. That's why the inside range wouldn't allow them. The owner told me that rifle rounds chew up his sheet metal back-stop too much."

"Look what we've come to in this damn state," Seth said. "Can't have guns that look like military weapons, so we have to go back to frigging nineteenth century lever-action rifles."

"It's not so bad," Trevor said.

"What, the dweebs in Sacramento? Seriously?"

"No, no, I meant the lever-action rifles," Trevor said. "Was reading an article about using them for urban warfare. They've got some serious advantages."

"Like what?" Seth asked.

"Weight and general handiness," Trevor said. "Hell, the .44 mag Winchester I just bought is way lighter than an M4. That means it's faster to bring to aim. It's also harder to jamb, can fire at a high rate for a non-autoloader, and it has a ten-round magazine."

"They take too long to load," Seth said.

"Yes, it takes more time to shove rounds through that side loading gate one at a time, that's true. But there are a couple of advantages there too, you know."

"Like what?" Seth asked.

"Well, for one thing, you can easily top them off, unlike the magazine on an M-4. Use five rounds and have a few seconds? Shove five more rounds in. On a Winchester, you can even shove a round into the chamber through the top when it's open. Remember that you have to carry all those clips with an auto-loader, and they take a long time to put cartridges in. With my Winchester, all I have to carry is the ammo."

"Yeah, okay, you've got a point," Seth said, "but at the end of the day, no modern army uses lever-action rifles."

"Oh, I didn't say they were my first choice," Trevor said, "but they can work out, and you can get really good with them after some practice."

Seth shook his head and pulled over in front of a big split-level house. Angel's smiling face greeted them as he waited on the sidewalk. He was slightly pudgy, with a round face and piercing eyes, medium length black hair hanging down almost to his eyes in the front. He went to the tail gate, opened it, and put his rifle and ammo in, then came around to the rear passenger side door.

"Hey, Angel," Seth said.

"How's it goin'?" he asked. "You guys are late."

"Only a little," Trevor said. "My fault."

"No problem," Angel said. "We'd just be waiting for Matt if you would've been on time."

"Well, there is that," Seth said. He looked back at Angel and snickered. "He bringing his little brother?"

"Nah, not this time," Angel said. "You guys get to fire these things yet?"

"No, been at work late every night this week," Seth said. "Hope I like the feel."

"I took mine to the indoor range and fired off a box of ammo," Trevor said. "Nice, but since it's so light, it kicks pretty hard."

"Well, I didn't have time," Angel said. "My dad needed me to help out with one of the apartments. The last tenants really trashed the place. They took the damn toilet, too. We walk into the bathroom and there's just a hole in the floor."

Trevor cracked up. "People are pigs."

"Seriously," Angel said. "You should have seen the back door. They put peanut butter on the screen of the Bellaire window. I had to use a toothpick to get it out."

Trevor laughed again, looking at Seth, who snickered.

"It's not funny, man," Angel said. "That was a pain in the ass."

"Why'd they do that, anyway?" Seth asked.

"My dad asked them to pay rent," Angel said.

"Geez, remind me never to be a landlord," Seth said.

"It's worth it. Most of the time your tenants aren't assholes."

Seth pulled into the driveway of a mid-century one-story house and honked the horn. A young man with long blond hair and a thick blonde beard rushed out with rifle and ammo box in hand, big grin on his face. He got into the rear driver's seat and slipped the rifle and ammo in the back. "Hey, losers," he said. "Mind if I smoke?"

"Yeah, what the hell," Seth said. "You're going to anyway."

Matt chuckled and opened his window a crack.

"You don't look so good," Angel said, giving him a sidelong glance.

"Got slammed with my uncle last night," he said, cigarette moving in his mouth. He lit it up. "Damn gin knocks me for a loop."

Angel laughed. "Again?"

"Yeah," Matt said. He took a big drag, and blew the smoke out his window. "Good thing I was with him. He wanted to go to that dive bar in Downtown Torrance to pick up some chick. I took his keys away. Man, was he pissed."

"Why does your mom put up with that guy?" Trevor asked. "He's got to be putting a bottle of gin away every day."

"He is," Matt said, taking another drag on his cigarette. "It's gonna kill him. My dad knows it, too. Only a matter of time. He told my mom he'd leave if she kicked Uncle Ned out."

"Would he?" Angel asked.

"I doubt it, but mom thinks he might," Matt said. "Ned supported the whole family after grandpa died. Raised my dad when grandma couldn't cope. My dad thinks he owes him."

"He probably does," Seth said. "I like the guy."

"I love him, but I wish he'd slow down on the boozing a little. We've got problems with addiction in my family. I look at him and it scares me."

"You think you're gonna have problems like that?" Angel asked.

"If I'm not careful," Matt said. "Kaylee's been bugging me about it. Made me promise that I'd only drink on the weekends."

Seth laughed. "Thursday night ain't the weekend."

"What are *you* laughing about?" Matt said. "You made the same promise to Emma. We both know how well that's been going."

Seth laughed again. "I know, look at us. Under the thumb of our women, and we ain't even married yet."

They all laughed as Seth got onto the freeway, heading for the Inland Empire.

"Hey Matt, I heard you had a little problem with Nathan," Trevor said, glancing back at him.

Matt laughed as he flipped his cigarette butt out the window. "Yeah, he got pissed, but he'll cool down."

"What happened this time?" Angel asked.

"Zoe," he said, twinkle in his eye. "I kinda blew it."

"Wait, that's the chick that you guys met at the coffee shop, right?" Trevor asked.

"Yeah, her and Megan," Matt said. "Megan's pretty hot, but she has a boyfriend. Zoe not so much. She looks okay if she dresses right, but she's dull looking. Dull to hang around with, too."

"Oh, I don't know," Seth said. "I think she's kinda cute."

"Nathan likes her, but he's never had a girlfriend. He doesn't know how to handle her, and she's losing interest fast."

"So we all know you nailed her," Angel said. "Where and how?"

"I wasn't planning on it," Matt said. "She needed a ride home because Megan flaked out on her. Her apartment is on the way to my place, so I took her. She wanted to talk, so we parked in that vacant lot off of 235th Street. One thing led to another."

Angel laughed. "You're a horn dog. How'd Nathan find out?"

"The bitch told him," Matt said. "She's not too bright."

"Aren't you afraid she'll tell Kaylee?" Seth asked.

"She doesn't know Kaylee, and I'm gonna keep it that way," Matt said.

"Enough of this crap," Trevor said. "What do you guys think about this scary stuff going on down at the border?"

"What, you mean the plane crash?" Seth asked.

"That wasn't a crash," Trevor said. "It was shot down. It's all over the web."

Seth chuckled. "The news media changed that story, remember? They said it was a hoax. The plane went down due to a mechanical problem."

"And you believe that?" Trevor asked.

"You guys ain't gonna talk politics again, are you?" Matt asked. "I'd rather talk about chicks and guns."

"And drinking," Angel said.

Matt laughed. "So sue me."

"No, *really,* there's something going on down there," Trevor said. "Unusual people are showing up. Crossing the border on its entire length, from Yuma to San Diego."

"Yuma is in Arizona," Seth said.

"It's right on the border," Trevor said.

"So what's unusual about them?" Angel asked, "and no comments about *wetbacks,* you assholes."

"They look unusual, and some people have overheard them speaking Arabic," Trevor said.

"Bullshit," Matt said. "That's conspiracy theory garbage. You need to stay off of those tin-foil hat message boards. Next you're gonna tell me that we didn't really land on the moon."

"That's a whole other subject," Trevor said. Seth turned towards him and snickered, rolling his eyes.

"My granddad worked on the moon launch," he said. "He knew some of the guys in Houston. It wasn't fake. That's just garbage."

Angel got a goofy smile on his face. "So Trevor, how do you feel about Nessie? Bigfoot? Spontaneous combustion? Area 51?"

"Ha ha ha," Trevor said. "There's more to things than meets the eye sometimes."

"I'm surprised *you* didn't mention Chupacabra," Matt said.

Angel laughed and punched him in the upper arm. "That's racist, man."

Seth laughed, looking over at Trevor, who couldn't resist laughing himself.

"All right, you've had your fun," Trevor said, "but I'll tell you something. Combat shooting isn't such a bad thing to know. What if we have an invasion coming?"

"The army will take care of it," Seth said.

"After all the cutbacks, the Army isn't what it once was," Trevor said. "You know this Administration."

Matt rolled his eyes. "Here we go again."

"No, really, man," Trevor said. "We might have to rely on ourselves."

"Then we're in deep yogurt," Seth said.

They continued the banter for the next hour, finally making it to the huge outdoor range, nestled against the hills in Grande Terrace.

"C'mon, guys, let's go," Seth said. "Our reservation was for five minutes ago."

"Coming," Trevor said. The others stepped it up, and they hurried to the office, lining up at the front desk.

"Reservations for the combat range," Seth said.

"Name?" asked the gruff old man behind the counter. He looked like an ex-cop.

"It's under Trevor Hall," Seth said.

"That's you?"

"No, sir, it's me," Trevor said, stepping up. He pulled out his driver's license.

"Weapons?" the old man asked.

"Three .44 mag Winchesters and a .357 Marlin."

The old man snickered. "Going in there with lever guns? Lot of that going around these days."

"Assault weapons ban," Trevor said.

The old man got a disgusted look on his face. "Yeah, it does narrow your choices a little, I guess. None of these are modified, right?"

"Modified how?"

"To fire by just cocking the lever," he said.

Trevor and Seth looked at the man like he was nuts, but Angel cracked up.

"Mucus McCain."

"I do believe that was *Lucas* McCain," the old man said with a smirk.

Angel laughed. His friends weren't getting it. "*The Rifleman*, you idiots. Chuck Connors. My dad loved that show. My brother and I came up with *Mucus* to mess with him."

"All right," the old man said. "So none are modified, then?"

"Nope, but it sounds like a good idea," Matt said. The old man rolled his eyes and shook his head, a slight grin showing.

"Hey, Gus, want to take these kids to the combat range?" the old man asked.

A man got up out of a chair behind the front desk and looked them over. He was about ten years older than them, wearing camo and sporting a crew cut. "Why do I always get the inbreeds?"

Angel laughed. Gus looked at him. "What's so funny, smiley?"

"Nothing," Angel said. He and the others followed Gus out the door and to the right, watching as he unlocked a gate about forty yards down. They took a path another hundred yards to a street with building facades.

"Okay, knuckleheads, whoever isn't shooting stands behind here," he said, pointing to a wall with a thick plate glass window. "That's the observation wall. And when you're shooting, don't shoot this direction. You do that, even by accident, and you'll be banned from the range. Got it?"

"Yeah, we got it," Trevor said, an excited look on his face. "This is gonna be a blast."

"No pun intended," Angel quipped.

Gus shook his head. "Who's first?" Gus asked.

"Let Trevor go first," Seth said. "He's the one who's nutso about this idea."

"I'm fine with that," Trevor said.

"Okay, normally we go thirteen rounds," Gus said. "For now, all you guys got to do is walk down the street and react. You'll see a target pop out. If it's a bad guy, shoot it. One shot only and move on."

"So I need to top up my magazine?" Trevor said. "Since I only hold ten?"

"Yeah," he said. "That's what puts the lever guns at a disadvantage during a tournament. But for you guys, don't worry about it. You don't have to worry about cover and tactics now either. If you do well, I'll give you some pointers on that, and talk to you about our classes."

Trevor took his rifle out of its case and set it on the table behind the observation wall. He loaded it, then stuck three loose rounds in his shirt pocket and walked out onto the street between the building facades.

"Ready?" Gus asked.

"Yeah." Trevor walked forward, rifle at the ready. There was a click. He turned and fired, hitting the target in a window dead center.

"Nice," Seth said.

Trevor continued walking until another target popped up. He whirled around, leveling the gun. It was a woman carrying a grocery bag. He lowered his weapon and kept walking. There was another click, and he fired, dead center again. He continued on through the course, topping off his magazine in the middle, only missing one target. He left the bolt open and walked back.

"That was great!" he said, setting his gun down.

"Damn, you're a natural," Gus said. "I guess I shouldn't have called you a knucklehead. Where are you from?"

"Torrance," he said.

Gus got a grim look on his face. "You know what happened there last night, right?"

"No," Trevor said. "We left pretty early this morning. Didn't bother with the news."

"Gang members went into North Torrance. Burned down several buildings, raped some girls, killed several people who resisted, and torched a bunch of cars."

"North Torrance?" Seth asked. "I can't believe we didn't hear about that."

"You live in North Torrance?" Gus asked.

"Nah," Angel said, "We're in the south-east part of town."

"I'm almost in Lomita," Matt said. "The line is just across the street from me. That's quite a ways from North Torrance."

"Well, you guys better watch yourselves around there," Gus said. "I know that area. My sister lives down by the airport. It's not that far from where the trouble was. Only four or five miles."

"Maybe it's a good thing we're learning to shoot combat, then," Matt said. "Who's next?"

"You," Seth said. "Go for it."

Matt nodded and took his gun out of his case. The boys took turns cycling through the course. Gus gave them all pointers, although he was most interested in Trevor's ability. They exchanged phone numbers with Gus at the end.

***

John woke up sweaty, intense morning light shining through the bedroom window of his rig. He felt for Sarah, but she wasn't there. "Sarah?"

"I'm out here," she said. "Want coffee?"

"Yeah," he said, climbing out of bed. "What time is it?"

"Little after eight," she called back.

"Why'd you let me sleep so late?"

"Eight isn't late," she said. "You're retired. Try to enjoy it a little bit."

He walked out, pulling on a sweatshirt. "Little chilly."

"It's not so bad," Sarah said, putting her newspaper down on the dinette table.

"You already been to the clubhouse?" he asked, sitting across the table from her.

"Yeah, I was there early," she said. "Woke up at five thirty and couldn't go back to sleep. I hate that." She got up and went to the coffee pot, taking a cup out of the cupboard and filling it. She brought it to the dinette and slid it to John.

"I could've done that, you know," he said, taking a sip. "But thanks."

"Don't mention it," she said. "What's on the agenda for today?"

"I have no particular plans," he smiled. "I'm retired, remember?"

There was some commotion outside. Loud talking, and then the alarm bell sounded.

"Crap, there must be a fire in one of the rigs," John said, standing up. He carried his coffee to the door and opened it, stepping out. Other people were coming out, looking around to see what the noise was about.

"Hey, John," Clem said, going down the steps of his rig. "Know what's happening? I don't smell any smoke."

"Nope, but the bell's still ringing," John said. "Let's go to the clubhouse."

Clem nodded and walked over.

"Wait for me," Sarah said, rushing down the steps and shutting the door behind her.

"What's going on?" Sid asked as he joined them with Yvonne by his side.

"Don't know," Sarah said.

Harry was already at the clubhouse with Nancy. Others were gathering around quickly as the bell continued to ring.

A middle aged man appeared, large and tan with a shaved head. He walked off the office porch with a bullhorn, looking out over the small crowd, and then stood on the planter wall in front of the clubhouse.

"You all hear me?" he asked.

"Yeah, Sam, we hear you," Clem said.

"Connie, shut the bell off," he said through the bullhorn. The bell stopped ringing.

"What's going on?" Sid asked. "Somebody get hurt?"

"There's a large Mexican gang heading this way on Highway 94," he said. "They just went through Barrett Junction. Killed the Sheriff and his deputy, took a couple of women hostage, and killed several other men in town."

"You think they're coming here?" Yvonne asked.

"We're off the road far enough, so we'll probably be okay," Sam said. "But you never know. No fires today. Try to keep the noise and the smells down. Then maybe they'll just pass us by."

"What are they driving in?" Sid asked.

"Big transport trucks, at least twelve of them," Sam said. "They look like military surplus."

There was a worried murmur in the crowd.

"I think maybe I'll find a good vantage point and keep watch," Sid said. "With my rifle."

"Don't you go trying to take these folks on," Sam said. "That might lure them here. They might kill all of us."

"I won't," Sid said.

"Take somebody with you," Yvonne said.

"No," Sid said to her. "Nobody else here knows those hills like I do, and they're treacherous. We don't need somebody rolling rocks down at a bad time."

Sam stared at him for a moment, then sighed. "All right, Sid, if you want to be our early warning system, be my guest, but don't tip them off that somebody's around. No pot-shots. Call us if you see them coming this way. Agreed?"

"Yeah, I agree," he said. "Any of you folks who are armed, load your guns and be ready, just in case."

"I was gonna suggest that," Sam said, "but be careful. Gunshots can be heard for a considerable distance. Don't be messing around."

"We ain't stupid, Sam," Harry said.

"Sometimes you are," Nancy said quietly.

"I heard that," Harry said. "Don't worry."

"How long till they get here?" Sid asked.

"Twenty minutes, give or take," Sam said. "If any of you is thinking of leaving, do it right now. Okay?"

A few people nodded in agreement, and then the crowd dissipated, most people looking really scared.

"Should we leave?" Sarah asked John as they were walking back to their rig.

"I couldn't get ready to leave in under twenty minutes," John said. "We've just gotta ride this out, sweetie."

{ 3 }

South Bay Mayhem

North Redondo didn't feel right.

"Be careful by the windows," Robbie said as they all got up the stairs. A couple of gunshots sounded.

"That's not very far away," Gil said. "Your dad have any guns around here?"

"He has a gun safe, but I don't have the combination," Robbie said. "If he bugged out in the motor home, he probably took most of his guns with him."

"I'll put the food and beer in the fridge," Steve said.

"Cool," Robbie said. "I'm gonna fire up my dad's PC and see if I can access the video cameras."

Justin sat on the couch in the living room and turned on the lamp next to him. Steve came in from the kitchen and sat on the other end of the couch, pulling out his phone.

"Is your sis someplace safe?" Justin asked.

Steve looked up from his phone. "She's in Hermosa. Said the vibe there isn't right. She's going up to her friend's house in Palos Verdes with a few other people."

"Wish I was with her," Justin said.

"You've got such a crush on Katie," Steve said. He smiled at him. "You should ask her out. She's made nice comments about you before."

"Really?"

"Yeah, really," Steve said.

"Bingo!" Robbie yelled from the front downstairs bedroom.

Steve and Justin rushed down there and joined Gil, looking over Robbie's shoulder at the PC display. The screen showed four video feeds. One in the garage, one pointing at the driveway, one pointing at the front door, and one pointing into the living room.

"My mom and dad can access this from wherever they are," Robbie said. "It'll link up to smart phones."

"Nice," Justin said. "They'll see us here eventually."

"Yeah, if they're okay," Robbie said.

"They're okay, man," Gil said.

"I'm gonna set my phone up," Robbie said.

"You guys want beer?" Justin asked.

"Think we're safe enough to hang out and drink here?" Steve asked.

"I suggest you don't get plastered," Robbie said. "Just in case. My dad's office downstairs has a big sliding glass door, and somebody could come into the back yard from next door on either side. Same with my mom's office in the back."

"There people in the other two units?" Steve asked.

"A couple lives in the front unit," Robbie said. "Rick and Diane. Original owners like my folks. The middle unit is a rental. Looked pretty dark when we came in."

There was another gunshot outside, startling all of them.

"Dammit, that was closer," Gil said.

"Sounded like the Galleria to me," Robbie said. "It's less than a mile as the crow flies." He pointed out the window towards the northeast.

"Should we go upstairs and watch the TV?" Steve asked. "Maybe the news has some chopper video. I keep hearing one out there every few minutes."

"Yeah, me too, circling," Robbie said. "I'll be up in a minute. I want to see how much food we have. My mom usually has a lot of Costco stuff in the deep freeze, out there in the garage."

"We don't have clothes over here," Steve said.

Gil laughed. "Yeah, you're right."

"Don't worry, when it's daylight we can go check things out," Justin said. "We might want to find a better place."

"See you guys up there," Robbie said. He went to the garage as the others went back upstairs. The chest freezer was just outside the door. He opened the lid. There was food, but not as much as usual. *They took a lot with them.* He shut it and went upstairs, going to the walk-in pantry. Lots of canned goods. Soups and other stuff. Lots of cereal. A case of beer. A bag of potatoes and a bag of onions. Then he looked in the fridge. It was pretty well packed. Some of the veggies looked a little old. *Why didn't mom dump them in the trash? How much of a panic were they in to leave? Why didn't they call me?*

Justin found the TV remote and clicked on the large flat-screen in the living room, then went to one of the local channels. The screen showed helicopter video of the Galleria. "Holy crap, look at this," he said.

Steve and Gil came in off the balcony. "Damn, that the Galleria?" Steve asked as he looked at the video on the screen.

"Yeah," Justin said.

Robbie walked in with a beer and sat down on the couch. "There's a lot of cops there."

The news readers came on the screen, the scene from the helicopter showing in a smaller square in the upper right-hand corner of the screen.

"There is mayhem in the South Bay at this hour," the woman news reader said. *"Police are trying to clear out the Galleria in Redondo Beach, which was under attack earlier by a large mob of gang members. The gangs left when the police arrived, but since many of the storekeepers had fled, the crowd took advantage and began carrying off merchandise."*

The male newsreader took over.

"This is the first night that the gangs have attacked west of Hawthorne Boulevard and south of El Segundo Boulevard. The police were ready but out-numbered. Several officers have been shot, along with several gang members."

A map graphic came up of southern California, with flame icons at the trouble spots. The woman news reader stood in front of it like a weather person.

"As you can see, there are problems in many parts of the South Bay," she said. *"Carson, Hawthorne, Inglewood, Redondo Beach, Harbor City, and parts of Wilmington are under attack at this hour. Mass looting, assaults, rapes, and murders. Some of the areas are so bad that police have abandoned them, urging residents still there to evacuate."*

The male commentator continued.

"The reasons for the sharply increased violence aren't clear. There have been bank failures and some unrest due to suspension of state entitlement payouts two weeks ago, but most of the late payments have been made as of yesterday. There are reports that agitators from outside of the United States are whipping up violence and leaving before the police arrive. We have no confirmation on that from official sources."

The woman took over again.

"Sources in Sacramento have indicated that the Governor is considering martial law in the areas hardest hit by the unrest. These areas include San Francisco, Oakland, Sacramento, Fresno, Ventura-

Oxnard, Los Angeles and many of its suburbs, Anaheim, Santa Ana, Irvine, and San Diego. The California borders with Arizona and Nevada have been closed."

"Geez," Steve said. "What would martial law be like?"

"Not good, but probably better than this," Robbie said.

"They'll come in and disarm the citizens," Gil said. "Wait and see."

"Your gun isn't going to protect you," Justin said.

"I'm not so sure you should be saying that," Steve said. "We might be dead right now if Gil didn't fire a shot over those gang-banger's heads. Remember?"

"Let's not argue," Robbie said.

There was a scream outside, and a couple of men laughing wickedly.

"Shit, that's right out front," Robbie said, rushing to the balcony.

"Wait for me," Gil said, grabbing his rifle.

"Diane!" Robbie yelled, watching two gang-bangers assault the middle-aged woman in the front section of the driveway, ripping her blouse halfway off.

"Rick!" she screamed. Suddenly the garage door rolled open, a German Shepard rushing out, snarling. It grabbed one of the men attacking her. The other man backed off, watching the dog chewing on the man's calf.

"Call it off, ese," yelled another gang banger, who ran up pointing a gun at the dog.

Robbie heard Gil's lever gun cock next to him. Gil aimed and fired at the man with the gun, hitting him square in the chest. He fell backwards, his head cracking on the pavement. Diane screamed, and Rick rushed out of the garage with a baseball bat, hitting the other gang-banger in the head, killing him instantly.

"I'm gonna burn you out!" shouted another gang banger who ran over. Gil got a bead on him and fired, hitting him in the side. He yelped in pain and looked Gil in the eye. "I'm gonna kill you!"

Gil cocked the gun and aimed again, but a car pulled up, and the wounded man was quickly pulled inside. The car sped away.

Rick looked up. "Thanks! That Robbie?" he yelled, helping Diane cover herself.

"Yeah," Robbie yelled back. "You okay?"

"I think so. We're leaving. Maybe you should too. They'll be back after this."

"Yeah, maybe you're right," Robbie yelled.

"Take care of yourself. Say hello to Frank and Jane when you talk to them."

"You know where they went?" Robbie asked.

"They told me they were going to Arizona in the motor home," he yelled. "Gotta go."

"Be careful," Robbie yelled back. He watched as they drove away in their Range Rover, running over the bodies of the gang bangers on the way out of the driveway. Gil and Robbie walked back into the living room, their hearts still pounding.

"You just put a big target on our backs," Justin said.

"He did the right thing," Robbie said. "Trust me. They were getting ready to rape Diane right in the driveway. They would've killed her and Rick if Gil wouldn't have shot at them."

"They might come back for us after that, you know," Gil said.

"They'll be back soon enough," Justin said.

"Don't be so sure," Steve said. "They have no idea how many of us are armed. We killed one of them and wounded another."

"Rick brained one of them with a baseball bat too," Robbie said. "The one their dog had ahold of."

"He dead?" Justin asked.

"Probably," Robbie said. "Rick ran him over on the way out the driveway."

"How many rounds you got left?" Steve asked.

Gil emptied his pockets. "Eleven loose rounds. Four left in the gun."

"Only fifteen?" Robbie said. "Dammit."

"Don't worry, we're pretty well protected here," Steve said.

"Except for those downstairs windows," Justin said. "They could start this whole place on fire."

"Right now they're worried about getting medical attention for their guy," Gil said. "They won't be back tonight. They'll go someplace where they can get free stuff without getting shot at."

***

Sid climbed up the hill, looking for a comfortable place to watch the road. He got to the ridge and rested for a few minutes, and then lifted his head. The stretch of road was below him. He could see a mile on either side. *Perfect.* He heard an engine coming right away, his heart starting to beat harder. The vehicle came into view. It was an old station wagon pulling a utility trailer full of stuff. Family inside. *Fleeing.*

The hot desert sun beat down on him, and it wasn't anywhere near the heat of the day yet. His phone vibrated. He pulled it out of his pocket.

"You in a good place?" Sam asked.

"Yeah," Sid said. "Just saw a family on the way out. Station wagon towing a trailer. *Grapes of Wrath,* man."

"You're liable to see a lot of them," Sam said. "Keep your head down. If the gang is still on the road, they'll be coming through any minute."

"I'll be watching. Are people ready down there?"

"I've seen a lot of people walking around with guns," Sam said. "John and Clem are up here with me, ready to fight. We'll be in trouble if we get a truck-full of bad guys here, though."

"Get more people up front and be ready," Sid said. "You've got signs up on the road. RV Parks full of retirees are easy pickings. They're likely to show up."

"Just don't do anything to help that along," Sam said.

"Don't worry." Sid said. He ended the call and went back to watching. Another car came by, loaded to the max with people and possessions, rounding the curve, driving a little too fast. Then an old Class C motorhome came into view, towing a small boat. Sid's heart pounded as he saw it, afraid that it was going to turn down their driveway. It didn't. Two more loaded cars drove by. One of them had steam coming out of its radiator. "Don't break down here," he muttered to himself, watching the old sedan until it was out of sight.

He wondered how Yvonne was doing at the trailer. He told her to get ready to leave, just in case. When she asked where they would go, he had no answers for her. He had just shrugged, leaving her nervous and scared, her Ruger Security Six on her belt.

A large truck rolled into view, military with a canvas cover over the back. *There they are.* Sid's heart hammered in his chest as he saw it approaching the RV Park turnoff. It went past that, continuing down the road. Sid sighed, trying to settle himself down. Another one. Same as the other, but with some bullet holes on the side, part of its canvas top ripped, exposing the tired men in the back. It went past the driveway. The next cars he saw were two sheriff's cars. They had men in white garb driving.

What were they doing with the sheriff's cars? Sid ran over the possibilities in his mind. Those patrol cars were a total bust. Probably had sensors in them, being tracked every inch of the way. Two more of the military trucks rolled into view, one of them slowing by the driveway. *No. They're looking at the sign.* The truck picked up speed again and continued on. Then a third sheriff's car appeared. This one had uniformed officers, both in the front seat and the back. *That isn't right.* It turned into the driveway. Sid fumbled with his phone in a panic, almost dropping it. He hit Sam's contact.

"Yeah, Sid."

"Phony Sheriff's car with four men on its way in. They were with the bad guys in the trucks. Be ready."

"Dammit," Sam said. "Okay. You're sure about this?"

"Yeah, I'm sure," he said. He ended the call and watched the road some more. There were no other trucks for several minutes. He called Sam back.

"I think that was all the trucks," Sid said. "I'm coming down. That Sheriff's car make it there yet?"

"No," Sam said, worried tone to his voice.

"You'll have to kill them. I'm on my way to the ridge above the park."

"Be careful," Sam said.

"You too." Sid slipped his phone back in his pocket and moved as quickly as he could to the ridge east of the RV Park. It wasn't far. He got into place and checked his rifle. *Wish I had the scope.*

He saw a flash of white on the road up to the front gate. The top of the police car, with its call letters. It pulled over, out of sight of the gate. The men got out, all of them holding AK-47s. Sid called Sam.

"They got out of the car. Gonna walk in. All of them have AKs. I can probably hit at least one of them. You got good people by the gate? Don't try to talk. Kill them."

"Roger that," Sam whispered. He ended the call. Sid got prone in his spot and aimed the rifle at the men. He could see Sam, Clem, and John in position, rifles aimed at the gate.

One of the fake deputies split off from the group, climbing up the side of the hill behind the office. Sid aimed at him. The other three walked right up to the gate. One of them rushed for the office door.

Sam moved out and shot him as he got on the porch. Sam and Clem opened up on the other two, hitting one, the other running. Sid pulled the trigger, hitting the man on the side of the hill square in the chest, his limp body sliding down. The running man was almost to the patrol car. Sid shot him, then put several rounds into the front of the car, steam rising from the hood. He took one more shot at the man lying close to the patrol car, hitting him in the back, insuring he couldn't make a call on the radio. Clem ran out of the gate, up to the man who was lying in the driveway, who looked up at him, trying to reach his gun. Clem shot him in the head.

Sid rushed down the hill, heart hammering in his chest, making it across the small meadow at the base of the hill, heading to the front of the park. He could hear women crying in some of the coaches.

"Sam, is the one on the porch dead?" he yelled.

"Yeah, dead where he fell," Sam said. "None of them got back to the patrol car, did they?"

"No," Sid said. "There was one coming up the side of the hill to bushwhack you guys. Nailed him. One tried to run to the patrol car. Nailed him too. Clem and John got the last one."

Clem walked up, John following. "That'll teach them," Clem said.

"The truck caravan knows where this place is," John said. "They're liable to be back. You know that, right?"

"Yeah, I know," Clem said. "We'd better get ready to high-tail it out of here."

"Can't go out that road," John said. "We'll run right into them."

"I'll go call the CHP and the local Sheriff," Sam said, rushing to the office door. Connie ran up and hugged him, tears streaming down her face.

Sid saw Yvonne rushing towards him and turned to her, his arm going around her waist as she sobbed against him.

"Are we going to leave?" she asked.

"I don't think we should," Sid said. John and Clem looked at him in disbelief.

"Why would we want to stay here?" John asked.

"To protect the people who can't leave," Sid said. "The people in park models. The people in trailers that haven't been road-worthy for years. Our friends."

Yvonne looked up at him, tears running down her cheeks. "You're a good man, Sid."

John and Clem looked at each other, then back at him.

"I'm not trying to shame you guys into anything," Sid said, "but I'm not leaving."

"Me neither," Yvonne said.

John sighed. "Okay, you've convinced me. How do we protect ourselves if they come back?"

"We need to discuss that," Clem said. "We've got resources. We know how to fight. We just need to figure out how to see them coming."

Sam came back out. "Heard what you said, Sid. Thanks. And you're right. We need a plan."

"Yeah, if Sid wouldn't have been in position to see that guy going up the side of the hill, at least one of us would be dead right now," John said.

"You get the CHP?" Clem asked.

"Connie was on the line with them when the battle was going on," he said. "She's talking to the local Sheriff's department now."

"Good," Clem said.

"I'll call a meeting," Sam said. "But first I'm gonna go take down my sign from the highway and lock the gate on the driveway."

"Got the sheriff's office, told them what happened," Connie said as she walked out of the office.

"Great," Sam said. "I'm gonna go get the sign."

"I'll help you, honey," Connie said.

"Want to go help too?" John asked Clem.

"You guys stay here and take a look at the ways up the side of the hills," Sam said. "Closing the gate won't keep men from walking in."

"I'll go back up on the ridge and take pictures with my phone," Sid said. "You can see everything from up there."

"Sounds like a plan," Sam said as he got into his Jeep. Connie got into the passenger side and they drove off.

"Are we gonna be okay?" Yvonne asked.

"Yeah," Sid said. "Why don't you come up on the ridge with me. A second set of eyes might help."

She nodded and they walked towards the back of the park.

{ 4 }

Watchers

Robbie was just about asleep on his mom's office couch when he heard a loud thump, then a scream. He peeked out the window into the side yard, seeing one kid helping another over the fence by the garage. He could hear crying. Somebody knocked on his door.

"Yeah," Robbie said. The door opened and Gil walked in with his rifle.

"What happened?"

Robbie snickered. "Some stupid kid tried to bust through the back garage door. Sounded like he broke his shoulder."

Gil cracked up. "Why didn't they just break the window there?"

"All these windows are visible from the surrounding houses," Robbie said. "The back garage door is the only one that's well hidden. Probably why my dad blocked it up."

"Think they'll be back?"

"Hell, Gil, who knows? I need to get back to sleep."

"Yeah, me too," Gil said. He left, closing the door behind him, going back to the front bedroom.

Robbie laid back down, looking at the ceiling, listening. There were still gunshots every so often, but in the distance. The gangs had gone home for the night. He drifted off, not waking up until morning, then threw his dirty clothes back on and left the room, climbing the stairs. Steve and Justin were sprawled out on the two couches in the living room. Justin stirred and looked over at him.

"Well, we survived the night, anyway," he said.

"Did you hear what happened around back last night?" Robbie asked as he headed into the kitchen.

"What time?"

"Had to be about three," Robbie said. He turned on the coffee maker and filled the water tank.

"Hell, I was dead to the world by then," Justin said. "Drinking a couple of beers put me out."

"Hey, guys," Steve said, sitting up and stretching. "What time is it?"

"Seven-thirty," Robbie said. The coffee maker groaned as it heated.

"So, what do we do today?" Steve asked.

"I'm going to my apartment to get the rest of my food and my clothes," Robbie said. "You guys can do the same if you think this place is safer."

Steve laughed. "My place is in a worse part of town than yours is, so I'll take you up on that."

"Me too," Justin said. "What about work? I might have to go in later."

"My job is closed up for now," Steve said.

"I've got to call in," Robbie said, "but I already know the answer. Nobody's going to expensive restaurants at night anymore. They've kept me off for the last week and a half, and things are getting worse, not better."

"You've still got the writing gig, though, right?" Justin asked.

"Yeah, but it doesn't pay much. If I can get out of the apartment, it would be enough to squeak by."

"I'll probably try to get to my parent's place eventually," Steve said. "I don't know if my car will make it there, though."

"They're in Tahoe, right?" Justin asked.

"Yeah," Steve said.

"Wonder how much of the state is messed up?" Robbie asked.

"You saw the news last night," Justin said. "Lots of areas are bad."

"I'd go join my parents if I could," Robbie said.

"Why don't you?" Justin asked.

Robbie chuckled. "I thought you watched the news last night. The border is closed."

"Oh, yeah," he said, sheepish grin on his face.

"Where's Gil?" Steve asked.

"Probably still asleep," Justin said. "That guy can sleep through anything."

"Oh, I don't know," Robbie said. "He's the only one of you guys who woke up last night when the mongoloid busted his shoulder."

A door opened downstairs, creaking.

Justin smiled. "Speak of the devil."

"Good, I'll whip up some breakfast, and then we can get going," Robbie said.

Gil thumped heavily up the stairs. "Hey, guys."

"Get enough beauty sleep?" Justin asked.

Gil smiled and flipped him the bird as he sat on the couch, leaning his rifle against the side.

"Had your pea-shooter with you all night, I see," Justin said.

"Damn straight," Gil said.

"We need more guns," Steve said. "Damn California laws make that next to impossible."

"Here it starts," Justin said.

"Just for the record, I agree with Steve," Robbie said, "but I'm not going down that rabbit hole with you guys right now. We need to eat and get the hell out of here."

The others nodded as Robbie went into the kitchen. He cooked up the rest of the eggs. They ate quickly, then went downstairs.

"We gonna go to our places separately and meet back here?" Steve asked.

"Yeah," Robbie said. "Save us a lot of time."

"Okay," Steve said, walking out to his car, which was the last in the driveway. He froze. "Hey, man, we got to move stuff out of the driveway. Looks like there was a field day in the front unit."

"Uh oh," Robbie said. He joined the others as they rushed out. There were boxes opened and rummaged through, a broken recliner, and various other things sitting in the driveway. The garage door was still open, stuff scattered all over the floor.

"Hey, man, something's missing," Gil said.

"What?" Justin asked.

"There were two bodies here, remember?" Gil asked.

Robbie looked at him, fear in his eyes. "Crap, you're right."

"We better check inside," Gil said. "Make sure nobody's camping out. Then we should move the debris inside the garage and lock the place up. This will be like a magnet tonight if we don't fix it."

"Yeah, you're right," Steve said.

"I'll go in first," Gil said, cocking his rifle. He entered through the garage door, heading into the hallway. There was stuff laying here and there. He opened the closet under the stairs. Nobody there. Then he checked the first-floor bedrooms. A mess, but no people. Robbie got behind him.

"We should take their food," he whispered. "They aren't coming back for a while."

"Let's finish the sweep first," Gil said. The front door was hanging open. Gill pulled it shut quietly, and locked the bolt. He put his finger to his lips and looked at Robbie, who nodded. They snuck up the stairs.

There was trash all over the floor in the living room and kitchen. The fridge was hanging open, much of the food sitting on the floor in front of it. The pantry was open, a few boxes on the floor, but most of the food looked okay. They continued into the master bedroom, ransacked with broken pictures sitting on the carpet. The bathroom was a mess, pill bottles all over the floor.

"That's it, nobody here," Robbie said. "I'll see if I can find extra keys."

"Good idea," Gil said. "This place is more defendable than your folks place in some ways."

"Mixed bag," Robbie said. "There's no sliding glass doors on the first floor. Only small windows. We could board them up. We could do the 4-by-4 routine at the back garage door and the front door. You can see up and down the street on the balcony. Decent place to shoot from."

"Yeah," Gil said. "I'll go help the guys move all the junk inside the garage. You want to handle the food?"

"If I can find an extra key, I'll leave the food here," Robbie said. "We can get it later if we need it."

"Okay," Gil said, rushing down the stairs.

Robbie put the perishable food worth saving back into the fridge and shut it. Then he searched for keys, looking on the walls for key hangers. Nothing upstairs. He went downstairs and looked there too. No dice. *Where would I hide them?* Bedroom. He went back up the stairs and started looking. Nothing in any of the dresser drawers. *Kitchen junk drawer.*

"Hey, Robbie, we got everything moved inside the garage," Gil yelled from the foot of the stairs. "Find keys?"

"Not yet," Robbie said, pulling open kitchen drawers. "Bingo!" There were several sets of keys in a drawer full of small hand tools, twister seals, chip bag clamps, and other assorted junk. He grabbed them, racing down the stairs and into the garage. He went to the back door and tried them, one after another.

"Hope one of them works," Steve said, coming in to watch.

"Me too," Robbie said, trying keys and then tossing them on the shelf next to the door. "Here we go," he said, holding up a key.

"Yes!" Steve said.

"Found it?" Gil asked.

"Yeah," he said. "Stand back while I close the big door, then we can go out this way and lock up."

Gil and Steve stepped inside and Robbie hit the garage door button. The door clattered down, and they went out the back door, walking through the wooden gate to the front yard.

"Where's Justin?" Robbie asked.

"He got a phone call," Gil said. "He's in the driveway."

They circled through the front yard to the driveway. Justin walked up to join them.

"What's up?" Robbie asked.

"My brother," he said. "Taking his family up north to the cabin in Bishop."

"You going?"

"Nah," he said. "They were asking if I could take one of their dogs."

"Fine by me," Robbie said. "Good early warning."

"What kind is it?" Gil asked.

"Pit bull," Justin said. "Scary dog, but a real sweetheart when you get to know him. His name's Killer."

"Why didn't they take him?" Steve asked.

"They had three other dogs. Not enough room, and you know how people feel about pit bulls."

"How's Killer gonna feel about us?" Gil asked.

"I'll introduce you guys. He's actually a good guard dog."

"Alright, bring him over, unless you want to go with your brother," Robbie said.

"His wife hates me," Justin said. "Feeling's mutual. He asked, but I don't want to crash their marriage."

"Okay, we ready to go?" Robbie asked.

"I am," Steve said. "I'll back out."

He trotted to his car. As he was backing down, a man in his early thirties approached from across the street.

"Who are you guys?" He eyed them, his muscles rippling under a tank top.

"My parents own the back unit," Robbie said.

"You're Frank and Jane's son?" he asked. "Got proof?"

"Driver's license?" Robbie asked.

"We don't have to listen to this," Justin said.

"Knock it off," Robbie said. "It's not bad to have somebody around who looks out for folks." He showed the license.

"Same last name," the man said. "I'm Cody. You see what happened to Rick and Diane?"

"I shot the two gang bangers that were messing with them," Gil said.

"I wasn't home last night," Cody said. "What happened?"

"Two gang bangers tried to rape Diane right in the driveway," Robbie said. "Gil shot one of them. Their dog grabbed the other one, then Rick brained him with a baseball bat."

"You said two gang bangers got shot," Cody said.

"Yeah, one came over and tried to save the other two," Gil said. "I shot him in the side, and then a car came by and picked him up. Should have shot him again. The creep probably lived."

"Is this the first time this street has been hit?" Robbie asked.

"No, but it's by far the worst, from the look of things," Cody said. "Your folks left after the first attack, but it was minor. It wasn't hard-core gang bangers. It was mostly kids from Lawndale. Where did your folks end up, anyway?"

"I haven't been able to raise them," Robbie said. "Rick said they were going to Arizona in the motor home."

"Good," Cody said. "Hope they're okay."

"Me too," Robbie said. "Where do you live?"

"Front unit on the corner there," he said, pointing across the street to a large condo complex on the corner. "I'm a reserve police officer. We kinda morphed into a militia. We helped with the problems at the Galleria last night. That was a mess."

"Yeah, saw some of that on TV," Gil said. "How late did you get home?"

"After five," Cody said.

"Oh, so you didn't see who took the bodies."

"I didn't notice any bodies when I drove up," he said. "Just the junk in the driveway. That's good. Means they're only coming after dark. They'll be back, though. You guys better either split or be armed."

"I'm taking off," Steve said from his car. "See you."

"Later, man," Robbie said. "I'll be back here in about three hours."

"What are you guys gonna do?" Cody asked.

"Get clothes and stuff from our apartments and come back," Robbie said. "All of us live east. Too dangerous there."

"It's not that safe here, either," Cody said. "Okay, I'll talk to you later. Got to get some shut-eye."

He walked back across the street.

"Maybe he's a good friend to have," Gil said.

"I don't like him," Justin said.

"So what else is new?" Gil said. "I'm outta here."

"Me too," Justin said. They all got to their cars and took off.

***

Sam was sitting on the porch in front of the RV Park office, rifle cradled on his lap, sipping coffee in the morning sun.

Connie came out of the office. "Honey, the CHP is out at the gate by the highway. They want you to let them in."

"Finally," he said. "Called them yesterday and they don't get here until this morning?"

"The sheriff never came yesterday either," Connie said. "Things must be really bad out there."

"I'll go let them in. Be back in a minute."

"Be careful," Connie said. "I'll tell the others you're going out there, just in case."

Sam nodded as he walked to the Jeep with his rifle in hand. He drove out onto the access road. It took nearly five minutes to wind his way to the gate by the highway. The CHP cruiser was parked, both officers standing next to it, watching him drive up.

"You took the sign down," the first officer said. He was middle aged with a weathered face and a crew cut. "You Sam? I'm Officer Ryan."

"Yeah, I'm Sam," he said. He looked at the other officer, who looked like a rookie, lanky with short blonde hair. He was staring silently.

"Oh, I'm Officer Patrick," he said. "Sorry."

"You want to come back or talk out here?"

"Come back, if that's okay," Officer Ryan said.

"Okay, let me swing this gate out of the way." Sam unlocked the massive padlock and swung the heavy gate to the side. "Drive through. I'm locking this after you."

"Good idea," Officer Ryan said. He got back in the car and drove through, leaving Officer Patrick standing there.

Sam ushered him inside and shut the gate, locking it, taking a last look up and down the road. "Okay, follow me." He got into his Jeep, made a K-turn, and took off towards the park. Officer Patrick got into the cruiser and they followed.

Connie, Clem, John, and Sid were all waiting at the gate for them. Harry was sitting on the porch, and a few others were milling around. Sam parked in front of the office, the CHP cruiser parking next to it.

"Look, it's Ponch and John," Clem said.

"We're never gonna live that damn show down," Officer Ryan said. He chuckled as he walked to the group, followed by Officer Patrick.

Sam walked over. "That's Connie. She's the one you talked to on the phone. Those other reprobates are Clem, John, Sid, and Harry. Guys, this is Officer Ryan and Officer Patrick."

"*You* guys took out the bad guys?" Officer Ryan asked.

"Yeah, we ain't as old and feeble as we look," John said.

"Speak for yourself, old man," Clem said, slapping his knee and laughing.

"You know those weren't Mexicans, right?" Sid asked. "They were Islamists with AK-47s."

"Yeah, we know," Ryan said.

"Damn heathens," Harry said, spitting on the ground.

"Okay, okay," Sam said. "What took you guys so long to get here?"

"You don't know what happened yesterday, do you?" Officer Patrick asked.

"Guess not," Sam said.

"The sheriff and his deputies are all dead," Ryan said. "Ambushed on the road. They might have been on their way here."

"What direction were they coming from?" Sid asked.

"Northwest, coming down highway 94," Ryan said.

"Dammit," Sid said. "Sorry that happened."

"Yeah, me too," Sam said. Connie began crying softly, holding onto Sam's arm.

"What now?" Clem asked.

"You folks aren't safe here, but you aren't safe on the roads either," Ryan said.

"So what do we do?" Connie asked.

"If it were me? Fortify your position here and ride it out," Ryan said.

"That's what I was thinking," Sid said. "We're working on that now. You notice the signs are gone."

"Yes, and that will help as long as that last convoy doesn't pass the word to others," Ryan said.

"Where's that convoy now?" Sam asked.

"We were tracking them with those two Barrett Junction Sheriff's cars, but they ditched them at the Jamul Indian Village," Patrick said.

"We've got units looking for them all around highway 94 and the major routes into San Diego," Ryan said.

"San Diego," Clem said. "What can they do there? With the number of trucks Sid saw yesterday, they've got under a hundred men. The local police would make short work of them."

"That's the main reason we've stopped by here," Ryan said. "Some of you are gonna stay put, right?"

Sam laughed. "Hell, all of us are gonna stay put. We've got too many people who can't leave. And like you said, the roads aren't safe."

"Good. You got anybody watching 94?" Ryan asked.

"Not every minute," Sid said. "We've talked about doing a rotation, though."

"I suggest you do that, both for your own safety, and to help us," Ryan said.

"So you want us to keep watch and communicate with you guys," Sam said. "I think we could live with that, but what's the end game?"

"We're trying to lock down San Diego," Ryan said. "We're having enough trouble taking on the enemy fighters who are coming in by sea and across the border near San Diego. If they open up a pipeline through the east here, it could be a real problem for the state. We could lose the whole damn region."

"Let's make a deal," Sid said. "We're low on ammo. Maybe you could bring us some."

"What do you need?" Ryan asked.

"We'll give you a list," Sam said. "Text it in to you."

"Okay, I'll have to run it by the brass, but I think they'll go for it."

"One other thing," Clem said. "If we waste these guys, we aren't going to be indicted for it, right?"

Ryan laughed. "Now who would do that?"

"The same creeps in the California State Government who've caused the problem in the first place with their loose borders and sanctuary cities," Clem said.

"You gonna spout off about sleeper cells again, Clem?" John asked.

"Damn straight," he said. "You heard about what's happening in LA County, right?"

Ryan sighed. "Yes, we've heard the rumors that outside agitators are stirring up the gangs to attack."

"I believe it," Patrick said.

"Me too," Ryan said. "I'm just a grunt. You know that, right? I can't tell you that no state official will ever get a wild hair up their butts and come after *vigilantes* like you guys. I *can* guarantee you that no law enforcement agency I know of would be willing to go after you guys for what you did yesterday, regardless of what the *diversity-at-all-costs* nutcases up in Sacramento think."

Sid laughed. "Well, that sounds solid."

"Look," Ryan said. "It's in your interest to watch the road, because you've killed four enemy fighters, and they might want revenge. You were gonna watch the road either way. All I'm asking is that you call us if you see anything."

"I'm just messing with you," Sid said. "I'm all for the plan."

"Me too," Sam said.

The others nodded in agreement.

"Thanks," Ryan said. "Would one of you guys take us back to the gate? We need to get moving."

"Sure," Sam said.

Sid and the others watched them walk away.

"Think we're gonna get attacked again?" Harry asked.

John, Sid, Harry, and Clem looked at each other. Sid shrugged. "Good question. Depends on what the first group was."

"What do you mean?" John asked.

Sid shook his head. "If that was a pilot group for a new invasion route, they'll end up killing all of us. They can't have anybody warning the authorities."

"Gee, that'll help me sleep at night," Clem said.

"When Sam gets back we need to have a meeting and set up that rotation," John said. "It needs to be 24-7."

Police Visit

R obbie drove slowly down Yukon Street to his apartment. The roads were filled with debris and broken glass.

His driveway was empty. None of the usual cars in the extra spaces in front. The door of the front ground-floor unit was hanging open. The rear ground floor unit past the three garage doors looked fine. He hit his opener and waited for the middle garage door to open, then pulled inside and got out, opening the trunk. He grabbed his tools off the shelves on the left wall, pushing them to the back of the trunk, then hurried up the stairs to his unit. His next-door neighbor cracked open her door.

"Robbie?" the young blonde woman asked. She was small and thin with a pretty face, about Robbie's age.

"Morgan," he said. "You okay? How about Brianna?"

"I'm okay, but last night was scary. Brianna's dad came and got her early this morning. I don't think she'll be back."

"Nobody came up here?" Robbie asked, looking down the walkway to the back. There were three more units behind his.

"No, thank God," Morgan said, stepping out. "Where did you go last night?"

"My folk's house in Redondo Beach."

"North Redondo or South Redondo?"

"North," Robbie said as he unlocked his door.

"Bad things happened there last night," she said.

"I know, we were in the middle of it," Robbie said.

"You were at the Galleria?"

"No," Robbie said, walking inside his unit. Morgan followed him. "We avoided that. It was a mess."

"Where did you have problems?"

"On my parent's street," Robbie said. He pulled a couple kitchen trash bags from under the sink and walked into the bedroom as Morgan walked in.

"Am I bothering you?" Morgan asked.

He stopped loading clothes into the bag and turned towards her. "No, not at all. Sorry, I can't stick around here very long."

"You aren't coming back, are you?"

"Probably not," he said. "You should go somewhere else. It's not safe here."

She looked at him, tears in her eyes. "I don't have anywhere to go. My parents live in Utah."

"You don't have any friends who live in a better location?" he asked.

"No, I didn't grow up here," she said. "I have some friends from work, but it's closed down now. I don't know how to get in touch with any of them."

"You were a bar tender, right?"

"Cocktail waitress," she said. "At one of the card clubs in Gardena. It's too dangerous around there now. All of them are closing."

"Geez," Robbie said, going back to packing. "This whole area is falling apart."

She sat on the couch and started to cry. "What am I gonna do?"

Robbie stopped packing for a minute and sat next to her, putting his arm around her shoulder. She leaned into him, calming down after a few minutes, then wiping her eyes and looking at him.

"Sorry," she said softly.

"It's all right," Robbie said.

"How come you never asked me out?" she asked. "I thought you would. You gave me the look more than once."

"You're out of my league," Robbie said. "I'm kind of a dork."

"No you're not," she said, smiling at him. "I would have gone out with you." She paused. "I *would* go out with you. I make it sound like you're dead or something."

Robbie laughed. "Well, not yet, anyway, but give it time."

"Don't say that," she said.

Robbie looked into her eyes, his heart pounding. "Look, you can come live with us if you want, until things settle down. It's me and three other guys, though."

"I don't want to impose," she said.

"You don't have anywhere else to go, though, do you? I don't mind."

"What are the others like?" she asked.

Robbie chuckled. "Typical South Bay kids like me. None of them are violent or mean, if that's what you're asking."

"Would they get upset if I was there?"

"No," Robbie said. "There's not much privacy. It's a three-bedroom condo. We do have some food though."

"Your parents aren't there?"

"No, they took off when things started to go bad. Left in their motor home. They're somewhere in Arizona right now."

"I'll bet you wish you were with them," she said.

"I do, but you can't get across the border anymore."

"Do you have brothers or sisters?"

"I have a sister, but she's up in Oregon," Robbie said. "I've got to get back to packing. You'd better start packing too."

"You sure it's okay?" she asked.

He stood and smiled down at her. "I'd love to have you there. Really. Now go get busy. I'll help you carry things down."

"I've got a CRV. It holds quite a bit."

"Good," Robbie said.

She got up and hugged him. "Thanks so much."

"Don't mention it," Robbie said. "One thing, though. This isn't all that much safer than here. The building is easier to defend, but that's about it."

"I know," she said, "but at least I'll be with other people." She scurried into her apartment. Robbie finished packing his clothes, and then grabbed other essentials. His toiletries, his books, some manuscripts, and other odds and ends. He went out with the first bag. Morgan already had two bags sitting by her door. She heard him and came out.

"Hey, you think I should bring this?" she asked, pointing to a revolver and a box of .38 rounds on the coffee table.

"Yes," Robbie said. "For sure. You know how to shoot it?"

"Yeah," she said. "I grew up in the country. My dad insisted that I bring that with me. I have several more guns, but they're all back home."

"Just keep it out of sight," Robbie said. "We've got a rifle. That's how we got out of here last night. Also shot a couple gang bangers in the condo when they were trying to rape the woman in the front unit."

"Oh, my God? *You* shot them?"

"No, my friend Gil," Robbie said. "We're almost out of ammo for that gun, though, and it's the only one we've got."

"Oh," she said, looking worried.

"I told you it's not really that safe there," Robbie said. "Not too late to back out."

"I still want to go," she said. "I'm almost done packing. Don't have that much. Should I bring food?"

"Yeah, definitely," he said.

"How about booze?"

"Yeah, bring that too if you want it," he said. "Not a good time to get ripped, though."

"I'll say."

Robbie nodded and rushed down the stairs. He dumped the bags into his trunk and went back up for his second load. He locked the door after he carried them out.

"That's all you have?" Morgan asked as she set two more bags onto the walkway.

"Yeah, but we took some stuff with us last night," Robbie said, walking past her. "I'll start bringing your stuff down after I stash this in my trunk."

She nodded and went back to work. Robbie came back up and grabbed two of her bags, taking them downstairs. Morgan had the last of her stuff bagged before he got back up. Her hair was brushed and she had a slight bit of makeup on when he got there. She saw him looking.

"Figured I should be a little more presentable," she said, an embarrassed smile on her face.

They each took bags and carried them down the stairs. Morgan opened her garage door and backed out the CRV.

"Wow, this does have a lot of space," Robbie said, watching her get out of the driver's seat. He heard a click, and the tailgate opened. She raised it the rest of the way and they loaded the bags.

"I've only got one more bag," she said. "I'll go lock up and bring it down."

"Okay, I'll back out. You can follow me. I'll make sure you don't lose me."

"Thanks," she said. He watched as she scurried to the stairs and rushed up.

"Hope I'm doing the right thing," Robbie muttered to himself as he backed his car out. He had it pointed in the direction of the street when Morgan got back down with her last bag. She came over to his driver's side window. "I'll pull over to the side and let you get in front of me."

"Good," Robbie said. "We're going to turn right on 182nd Street, take that to Inglewood Avenue and make a right, then take a left on Grant."

"Okay," she said. "I kinda know the area. A guy I was dating lived on Matthews."

"If there's a blockage, just follow me," Robbie said. "We had to go way out of the way last night because of that mess at the Galleria. Should be fine now, but you never know. They might have some streets closed for investigations."

"All right." She got into her car and made a right turn on Yukon, pulling over to the side right away. Robbie passed her and she fell in behind. There weren't any problems on the way, but there were lots of spent flares lying on the road, especially at 182nd and Kingsdale, the southern gateway into the Galleria.

Robbie was back to the condo before his friends. He pulled into the garage and got out, motioning for Morgan to pull into the visitor parking place. Then he got in front of the CRV and guided her so she was hard up against the gate.

"I take it you don't want anybody going through that gate," she said as she got out.

"You got it," Robbie said, moving to the back of her vehicle.

"Nice looking building," she said. "These are expensive. Your folks must have done all right."

"I'm surprised they've stayed here, frankly," Robbie said as he helped her pull bags out of the back of the CRV. "They could afford more. They like this neighborhood because it's walkable, and because it's close to the freeway." He unlocked the front door and opened it, moving the bags inside, stacking them in front of the stairs.

"What makes this place defendable?" Morgan asked as she closed her tailgate.

"It's harder to rush back here, especially when the others get here and park in the driveway. They staggered last night so you couldn't walk back. It's not perfect, though. There are sliding glass doors in the downstairs bedrooms. Wouldn't be hard to break those out. Just a sec."

He went back out the door and into the garage, hitting the button to close it. He entered through the side garage door, meeting Morgan by the foot of the stairs.

"What about your stuff?" she asked.

"I'll get it later. Not sure where to put you."

"Where have you been sleeping?"

"It's only been one night. I slept in the back downstairs bedroom, just in case anybody decided to break in down there. I guess I should take my parent's room eventually, but maybe you should be in there now."

"It's upstairs?" she asked.

"Yeah," he said. "Let's get the perishables up there. Oh, and there's a deep freeze in the garage if you have frozen stuff."

"Most of the food I brought *is* frozen. Why don't you show me where the freezer is? We'll load that before we go up."

Robbie nodded and walked her down the hall.

"You guys have a cat?" she asked, looking at the cat box on the hall floor in front of the laundry room.

"My folks have one. Mr. Wonderful."

Morgan laughed. "Great name. Is he here?"

"No, he's with them in the motor home," Robbie said. "I should empty out the cat box and take it outside. Here's the garage door." He held it open for her. She opened the top of the freezer and stashed her stuff in there.

"Wow, lots of Lean Cuisine," Robbie said.

"Yeah," she said. "I'm lazy when I live by myself. Wow, there's a turkey in here."

"Yeah, there's lots of stuff in there," Robbie said. "More upstairs, and some in the front unit too."

"Front unit?"

"Oh, forgot to mention that. That unit got ransacked last night, after the attempted rape I told you about. We picked things up, found extra keys, and locked it back up again. The fridge and pantry have food in them."

"They coming back?" Morgan asked.

"I have no idea," Robbie said. "Judging by what happened last night, if they have elsewhere to go, we won't see them."

"Geez." She closed the top of the freezer and set the empty bag beside it. "Show me the rest of the downstairs."

Robbie nodded and took her back inside. "Laundry room."

She opened the louvered door and looked inside. "These are high-end machines."

"Yeah," Robbie said as he opened the door to the back bedroom. "This was my mom's office. The couch makes into a queen bed, but I just slept on it closed last night."

She looked inside. "There's the sliding glass door you were talking about. She walked over and moved the curtains aside. "The fences on the sides of the yard aren't very high."

"No, they're not," Robbie said. He led her to the front bedroom. "This was my dad's office. Gil slept in here last night. He's the one with the rifle."

"That sofa doesn't look very comfortable."

"It's not as bad as it looks," Robbie said. "My dad's PC is connected to the video cameras."

"Oh, you've got video, eh?" Morgan said. "Not a bad thing."

"We probably should move more of the cameras outside. Right now there's one outside the garage, one inside the garage, one pointing to the front door, and one in the living room that covers a lot of the upstairs."

"Your dad set it up so he could keep an eye on the place while they're gone," Morgan said. "My dad had a setup like that. He could access it over the web with his iPad."

"Yeah, same thing here," Robbie said as he led her up the stairs.

"Oh, this is nice," she said. "Look at that big balcony. Nice dining room, too."

"Not bad," he said. "Steve and Justin slept on those couches, as you can see." Blankets were still sitting on them.

"Nice kitchen," Morgan said. "It's got the electric ovens and a gas range. That's the hot setup." She walked around, seeing the door at the far end. "That the pantry? I have some stuff to go in there."

"Yeah," Robbie said.

"Be right back." She went down the stairs, coming up with two bags, setting one by the fridge, and carrying the other to the pantry door. She opened it. "Wow, nice." She loaded in her food.

"Yep," Robbie said. "My mom raved about that pantry when they moved in. Good if you go to Costco a lot."

"How long have they owned the place?"

"Sixteen years or so. They were the original owners."

"You lived here for a while, then?"

"Couple years," Robbie said. "Maybe that's why I picked the back bedroom last night. Used to be mine. Sis was in the front bedroom."

"Where did you live before here?"

"Torrance," Robbie said as Morgan put food in the fridge.

"Why'd they move here? Torrance is so close. It has bigger houses and better parking too."

"They were downsizing," Robbie said. "My dad was tired of driving surface streets all the way to the freeway from south Torrance, too. He worked in El Segundo."

"Yeah, I know people who hate the South Bay because of that."

"I guess," Robbie said. "It's kind of nice not having freeways so close, as far as I'm concerned. Never liked it as much here as I did in South Torrance. That's still my stomping ground."

"To each his own," she said, closing the fridge doors. "What else?"

"There's a powder room here," he said, leading her back into the living area. "And here's the master." He opened the door.

"Like that shower," she said, looking into the bathroom, to the right of the door. Then she walked into the main part of the bedroom. "This is nice. Nobody's using this?"

"No," he said, "You could sleep in here if you want. It's the most private place we have."

"Not a chance," she said. "You should move in here. It's your place."

"Maybe," Robbie said. "We'll see. We've got some planning to do after the others get back."

"Okay," she said. "If they don't want me here, I'll find someplace else."

Robbie looked at the concern on her face. "Like you just said, this is my place. You can stay if I say so. Don't worry about it."

"You're nice," she said. "Wish you would have asked me out."

His face turned red.

"Are you embarrassed?" she asked, smiling at him.

"A little, I guess," he said. "I was never very good with girls."

"You're just a little shy," she said.

"Oh, forgot about one thing. You okay with dogs?"

"I love dogs," she said. "Why?"

"One of my friends is bringing his brother's dog. Supposed to be a good watch dog. It's a Pit Bull, though. You okay with that?"

"Of course," she said.

They left the master bedroom, going back into the living room. There was a harsh knock at the door. Robbie shot Morgan a worried glance, and then rushed to the balcony, looking down at the front door. There were two police officers there.

"Hi," Robbie said, trying to sound friendly. "Be right down."

"Thank you, sir," one of the cops said. Robbie rushed down the stairs, Morgan right on his heels. He opened the door. "Come on in."

"Thanks," the first officer said. He was a large Hispanic man. His partner was a white woman. Her eyes darted around as she came in.

"Sorry to bother you," she said.

"No bother at all," Robbie said.

"You the owner?" the male officer asked.

"No, it's my parent's place. They're off in their motor home. Arizona, last I heard."

"Do you know the couple who own the front unit?" the female officer asked.

"Rick and Diane," Robbie said. "Yes. They fled last night after some gang-bangers attacked them. They coming back? We picked things up around their house and locked the doors up for them."

The two officers looked at each other.

"The house got ransacked?" the male officer asked.

"Yes, sometime overnight," Robbie said. The officers looked at each other again.

"Oh no, what happened?" Robbie asked.

"They were murdered last night," the female officer said. "Right before the on-ramp to the 405, on Artesia."

"Crap, they drove by the Galleria?" Robbie asked. "Bad place to be around last night."

"Yes, but we have reason to believe that they were followed from this location," the male officer said. "One of the gang-members expired later in the evening. He had a bullet wound to the side. Bled out."

"Why do you think they followed Rick and Diane from here?"

"The deceased gang member had keys to the condo on him," the female officer said.

"They had a dog with them," Robbie said. "Big German Sheppard."

"Dead at the scene," the male officer said. "Same gun that killed the couple."

"Is there next-of-kin in the area?" the female officer asked.

"Don't know, sorry," Robbie said. "I didn't know them very well; only lived here for a couple of years, when I was a teenager."

"I see," the male officer said. "Anybody living in the middle unit?"

"That's a rental," Robbie said. "When we got here, it looked deserted."

"When did you arrive?" the female officer asked.

"Last night," Robbie said. "My friends and I had to leave my apartment in North Torrance. This was the only place we could come."

"It's not much better here than it is in North Torrance," the male officer said. "Don't go out after dark. Protect your girlfriend, too. They're on the prowl for young, attractive women."

"Will do, officer," Robbie said.

"Okay, you two take care," the female officer said. They walked away. Robbie shut the door.

Morgan giggled. "Girlfriend?"

Robbie shot her a sheepish grin. "Correcting them would have been kind of a long story. I wanted them out of here before they asked too many questions about the gang bangers Gil shot last night."

"It's okay," she said, resting her hand on his shoulder as he turned towards the stairs. "I should be so lucky."

Robbie's heart raced. He turned back to look at her face. "Let's go have something to eat. I'm starving."

They walked up the stairs.

{ 6 }

Park Rules

It was nearing dusk at the Dulzura RV Park.

"You about ready?" John asked, standing next to the kitchen counter.

Sarah came out of the bedroom, putting in earrings as she walked. "Yes, I'm ready," she said. "Is there going to be drinking at this thing?"

"That again," John said. "I haven't had a drop since this mess started. We all need to stay straight."

"Good, that's what I wanted to hear," she said. "Let's go."

They left the motor home, walking towards the clubhouse. Sid and Yvonne joined them.

"Hey, John," Sid said. "How you doing?"

"Nervous," John said.

"Me too," Sarah said.

Yvonne looked at them, nodding in agreement.

"You've got a little bit of sunburn," Sarah said, looking at Yvonne's reddish forehead. "Didn't think that happened."

Yvonne laughed. "Why, because I'm Indian?"

"Well, yeah," Sarah said. "Sorry, that wasn't nice."

"Oh, please," Yvonne said. "You know I'm not one of those. It was a valid question."

"Sid kept you up on the mountain too long," John said.

"It was my fault. I should have brought my hat," Yvonne said. "I'll remember next time."

Harry and Nancy joined them. "Hi, folks," Harry said. Nancy nodded and smiled.

"Where's Clem?" John asked.

"He's already inside," Harry said. "Saw him walk by a few hours ago. Said something about helping Sam."

The group entered the clubhouse, finding seats at the table a couple rows away from the stage. There was a podium with a microphone to the right side. A buffet sat on tables against the right wall, the smell of chili and enchiladas filling the room.

"Food?" Sarah asked. "Didn't know they were having that. Glad we didn't eat before we came."

Connie walked out carrying an industrial sized bag of tortilla chips and a tub of salsa. "Come and get it, everyone!"

"Thanks!" Sid said in a loud voice, standing, taking Yvonne by the hand. They headed for the table, others following them.

"No beer," Harry said. "Probably a good idea."

"Yeah," John said. They got in line for food. "Too crazy to be walking around drunk."

Sarah locked arms with him and looked up, a comfortable smile on her face.

The room was filled with conversation and laughing as everybody sat eating their food. Sam and Clem walked in the side door and got into line.

"There they are," John said, nodding. "Wonder what they're up to?"

"We'll probably find out in a few minutes," Harry said.

"Damn, these enchiladas are really good," Sid said. "I might have to go for seconds."

"Wait till everybody has had some," Yvonne said.

He grinned at her. "Yes, mom." Yvonne elbowed him, shaking her head.

"You like it?" Connie asked as she walked up, her pretty black hair swaying as she looked around the group.

"Well, as you can see, I hated it," Sid said, pointing to his empty plate.

"Have some more," Connie said. "We have plenty. Haven't even brought it all out yet."

"Thinking about it," Sid said.

"Go ahead, honey," Yvonne said.

He grinned and took his plate back to the line. A few others were getting up for more too.

"How are you holding up?" Nancy asked. Connie shrugged.

"I'm scared, but I feel safe with Sam," she said. "He's had military training."

"Really?" John asked. "Which branch was he in?"

"He was a Navy Seal," Connie said.

"Wow, really?" Harry asked. "I had no idea."

"Hey, folks," Clem said, walking over with a plate of food. Sam was right behind him.

"Get what you needed?" Connie asked.

"Sure did," Sam said. "We'll put it all up tomorrow. It's wireless. We'll need a couple of repeaters, but I was gonna do that anyway to improve the Wi-Fi."

"You guys got a surveillance system?" Harry asked.

"Yep, that's where we went," Clem said. "I'm anxious to see how the big one works."

"Big one?" John asked.

"We needed a way to see down the access road without extending the Wi-Fi way out there," Sam said. "We bought a really nice camera on a gimbal. It's got a zooming SLR-quality lens, and we can point it from a PC or tablet."

"Wow," Harry said. "Pricey?"

"That baby cost more than the other twenty-four cameras combined," Clem said. "It also has some night vision capability. This stuff has gotten a lot better since I retired from my home security business."

"I'm glad you still had the connections," Sam said. "If we wouldn't have gotten this stuff wholesale, it would've broken the bank."

"So, you got 25 cameras?" John asked.

"Yeah, but twenty-four of them were part of a kit. The big one is standalone, and it can swivel around to cover almost all of the park."

"Where you gonna mount it?" Harry asked.

"Flag pole in front of the office," Sam said. "We can hard-wire it and switch it between wireless and the hard-connection."

"It won't see all the way to the highway, though, will it?"

"Nah, Harry, just down to the last bend," Clem said. "But that's eight hundred yards. It'll give us some early warning."

"We got the alarm for the gate," Sam said. "We'll know if somebody crashes it."

"How are people gonna come and go?" Harry asked.

"We'll work that out," Sam said. "It was the main reason for the meeting."

Sid came back over with a plate full of food.

"Geez, you gonna eat all of that?" Yvonne asked.

"I figured you'd want some too," he said.

She sighed. "You're always trying to make me fat."

"We eat light most of the time," Sid said. "Besides, climbing around in the hills and being in the sun all day takes a lot of energy. You should eat a little more."

"Oh, all right," she said, picking up her fork. She joined Sid, eating enchiladas, rice, and beans. "This is really good, Connie. You make it yourself?"

"No, I got it from my sister's restaurant."

"You bought all this?" Sid asked. "Must have been expensive. You should take up a collection."

"We got it for nothing," Connie said. "They had to close the restaurant temporarily because of the trouble. This food would have gone bad if she wouldn't have given it to us."

"Oh," Sid said. "So we're helping out." He chuckled. "Glad to be of service."

Yvonne slapped his thigh. "Really?"

Connie laughed. "We owe you, Sid. Not only did you help in that battle earlier, but you convinced the others to stick around."

"I didn't convince nobody," Sid said. "I made a decision, and the others made the same decision."

"That's true," Sam said, "but you were the catalyst."

"Ah, shucks," Sid said. Yvonne slapped his thigh again. "What?"

"I can't take you anywhere," she said, shaking her head. "That's what I get for marrying a crazy old Indian."

"Says the squaw," Sid said.

Harry, Clem, and John laughed. Sam almost spit out his food.

Yvonne glanced at Nancy, Connie, and Sarah, then shrugged. "I guess it's not so bad," she said.

"I'd better get this meeting started," Sam said. "That microphone turned on?"

"Not yet, honey," Connie said. "You ready?"

"No, but that never stopped me before." He wiped his mouth with his napkin, took a big drink of soda, and got up.

"I'll go turn it on," Connie said. She walked onto the stage and went behind the wall as Sam got behind the podium. He tapped the mic. Nothing.

"Just a sec, sweetie," Connie said. "There, now try it."

He tapped on the mic, and it sounded into the room. "Got it."

"Good," Connie said. She came off the stage and sat back down next to Sarah. A hush came over the room.

"Can you all hear me okay?" Sam asked.

"I can hear you in the back of the room," an old man said from near the door.

"We hear you fine up here, too," John said.

Sam smiled. "Welcome. Thanks for coming."

"Thanks for the food," Sid said.

"You're welcome. I won't keep you for too long. We have a few things to discuss. Hopefully we can come to a consensus."

"We're all ears," Harry said.

"Good," Sam said. "I bought some hardware today. A set of 24 fixed video cameras, one high-end zoom camera, and an alarm system for the gate down by the highway. First of all, does anybody have objections to the cameras being placed around the park?"

"Why would we care about that?" Sid asked.

"Some might think it's an invasion of privacy," Sam said. "If any of you have concerns, please speak up now and we'll address them."

"Normally I would object," said a middle-aged man in the middle of the room, "but at this point, I think they're helpful. Will they stay up after this situation is over?"

"That's a good question, Josh," John said.

"I propose that we only use them during these times, however long they last," Sam said. "I might not take everything down afterward, but at the very least I'll turn them off, and have the display visible so everybody knows they're off. Good enough?"

"Good enough for now," the man said. "Thanks."

"Any other concerns?" Sam asked.

"Are we still going to set up a rotation of sentries?" Sid asked. "Humans are better than cameras."

"I'll throw that open to the group," Sam said. "My suggestion will be that we do set up a rotation, at least for now."

"I think it's vital," John said.

"Me too," Sid said. "We have better eyes and ears, and we can react."

"Anybody object?" Sam asked.

"Do we all have to participate?" an older man in the back asked. "Some of us are in better shape than others."

"I think we can get enough volunteers without having to compel everybody," Sam said. "We all know there's a mixture of people here. I can put a signup sheet on the table right inside the door of this room. Sound okay?"

"I think that's a great idea," Harry said.

"Me too," Sid said.

"Okay," Sam said. "Moving on. The alarm on the gate. We can restrict use of that to nighttime, or we can have it on all the time and set up times for people to be able to leave the park. What do you guys think?"

"I think we ought to have it on all the time for the next couple of weeks," John said. "We can go to nighttime later if things settle down."

"If we go for full time, how often would we have open times for people to leave?" asked Josh. "Some of us still work."

"I'll let you in and out to support your work schedule, Josh," Sam said. "Same with the others who are still working."

"Thank you," Josh said.

"How about guns?" Sid asked. "We've been carrying them since things went sideways. I know if scares some people. Do we want to talk about any guidelines for that?"

There was a murmur through the room.

"I wasn't aware that anybody was afraid of it," Sam said.

"I don't like it," said a middle-aged woman in the back, "but I'll go along for now. After things get back to normal, I think we should go back to the way it was before."

"I'm fine with that, Erin," Sam said. "Anybody else have any comments about that?"

"People who have been drinking should not be able to carry guns," Josh said. "I think we can all agree on that."

Sam looked out over the crowd. "Well, what do you think? I'm okay with that, but I'm not going to get put into the role of law enforcement. You folks will need to police yourselves. Friends and spouses."

"I'm not sure that's enough," Erin said. "You can post rules so we're all clear. That will make it easier. Then any citizen in the park can bring up the rules we've all agreed to if they see problems."

"I think that's fair," John said.

"Me too," Sid said. "We shouldn't be drinking right now anyway, frankly. Not until the state gets back to normal. Never know what might happen."

"Okay, then we'll draft up some guidelines and post them," Sam said. "Who will volunteer to help with the drafting?"

Several people raised their hands, including Erin, Josh, Harry, and Connie.

"I'm okay with this," Sid said, "but we need to vote on the final result before it goes into effect."

"That could tie things up too long," Erin said.

"No it won't," Sid said. "It's only fair. Some of us are more likely to get into gun battles than others. I won't put myself at risk with regulations that don't make sense during the present time."

"So you're not going to follow the rules if you don't like them?" Erin asked.

"I didn't say that," Sid said.

"You almost did," Josh said, "but I agree with what you propose."

"Anybody object on the vote?" Sam asked.

Nobody spoke up.

"Okay, we'll use the volunteers to draft the rules, and everybody will have the chance to vote on them. That's all I had to say. Anybody else want to discuss anything?"

"I think we should continue the ban on campfires for the time being," Sid said. "That smoke can be seen and smelled for miles."

"What does everybody think about that?" Sam asked.

"Fine by me," Erin said. "I don't like the smell anyway."

"Anybody object?"

Clem raised his hand. "I'm fine with it for now, but would like to see the restriction lifted after the trouble is over. Just like the other things we're putting in place."

Erin sneered at him but stayed silent.

"Anybody object to that?" Sam asked.

Nobody spoke up.

"Okay, I'm done, then, unless there's anything else," Sam said. "I'll get out of your hair. Eat up. We've got more food in the back."

The group gave Sam a round of applause as he came off the stage. He joined Connie at the table.

"Have some more food, dear," Connie said.

"Don't mind if I do," he said.

"Sorry about that last one," Clem said softly.

"What?"

"Pushing back at Erin on the campfires. I don't want that control freak getting too many rules set up here. She's hell on wheels."

Connie giggled. "Yeah, I agree."

"Bottom line, after we get past this, I'll go back to trying to get overnight business," Sam whispered. "People on vacation want campfires. She don't like it, she can leave."

"Here here," Clem said.

"Well, I'm going back on the hill for a while longer," Sid said. "It's almost dusk. If we're gonna get hit again, it'll probably be after dark."

"Want me to go, honey?" Yvonne asked.

"You don't have to tonight," he said, "but keep your phone next to you at all times with the ringer on, all right?"

"All right," she said.

"I'm gonna watch the front gate area," Clem said. "Maybe patrol it as far as the bend."

"Both of you guys watch for rattlesnakes," Sam said. "Getting to the season."

"Will do," Clem said. He got up to leave. Sid did the same, and they walked out the front door together.

"Well, Sid, what do you think?" Clem asked.

"I think we'll be lucky if we don't get hit tonight, and if we don't get hit tonight, we probably won't get hit at all."

"Hmmm," Clem said. "It all depends on if somebody passed the word about us. If our location is known and passed around, we might not get hit until the next convoy comes through. That could be several days or a week."

"Or now," Sid said. "See you. Going back up the hill."

"Watch your step," Clem said, "and watch for rattlers."

Sid nodded and walked away. Clem watched him for a moment, then headed to his coach to get his gun.

***

It was nearly dark as Seth parked in front of the South Redondo apartment building. The damp ocean air was coming in, fog building, making halos around the streetlamps of Prospect Avenue. There was gunfire in the distance, causing his heart to beat a little bit faster.

"It's getting closer," he muttered to himself as he left the car, heading up the sidewalk past condos and apartment buildings. He hoped the cigarette smell was gone. He didn't smoke, but he'd been around Matt all day long. Emma didn't want him smoking, and bullied him into quitting. *No, I chose it.* He shook his head, fear and anger flaring and receding as he walked to the door of apartment G. He knocked.

"Come in, I'm still getting ready," Emma said from inside. He opened the door and walked in.

"You shouldn't have the door unlocked," Seth said. "You know how things are now."

"It's not bad here," she said, coming out, drying her thick, golden blonde hair. She was wearing a white terry-cloth robe which was starting to come open, her ample cleavage showing.

"Oh, geez," he said, walking towards her. She looked at him, ready to give him a peck, but he moved in and kissed her hard, his hands going inside the robe.

"Wait," she said, pulling back from him. "You don't like to be late, remember?"

"It's just another stupid party with my friends," Seth said, coming in for another kiss. "You don't like to be with them that much anyway."

She sighed, giving in and kissing him back as his hands pulled the robe off her shoulders, her shapely figure causing Seth to moan. "I've been waiting to see you all day."

"You've been with Matt, from what I smell," she said. "You didn't smoke, did you?"

"No, I didn't," he said. "Really."

She backed up and looked at him, trying to see past his eyes, poised to get angry. Seth kissed her again, harder, and she melted. "Okay, let's make it quick." He led her into her bedroom and shut the door behind them.

Afterwards they lay panting, still in embrace.

"Wow, you were really into it," Seth said, looking over at her. "You were wanting that as much as I was."

She looked into his eyes, face turning red. "Maybe," she said softly.

"Why does it embarrass you? This is what couples do."

"I know," she said. "I can't help it."

Seth sat up and chuckled. "Well, that's part of your charm. When you give in it's like a dam breaking."

"Shut up," she said. "Let's get ready to go."

"Where are your roommates?" Seth asked as he stood to get dressed.

"I don't know," she said. "They didn't leave a message or anything, but most of the food is gone. Makes me mad. I bought some of it."

"They flew the coop because of the problems," Seth said. "Maybe we should too."

"And where would we go?"

"I don't know," Seth said. "My grandparent's cabin, maybe."

"Up in the mountains?"

"Yeah," he said. "Why not?"

"I suppose your friends would come too," she said.

"Yeah, including Kaylee," Seth said.

"Well, that's something, I guess. When are the rest of them going to get girlfriends?"

"Angel has been going out with some chick, but he never brings her around," Seth said.

"Maybe that's why he's been losing weight."

"Yeah, maybe. Might just be baby fat falling off too."

"I doubt it," she said. "He's too old for that now."

"He's a late-bloomer," Seth said.

"What about Trevor?" She shot him an eye-rolling glance. "Just kidding."

"Why do you hate him so much?" Seth asked.

"I don't know," she said. "His condescending attitude. He thinks he's smarter than everybody else."

"Yeah, he does have that a little," Seth said.

"A little?"

"Okay, a lot," Seth said.

"Where's this party tonight?"

"Some guy who Matt knows has a house up above Rocketship Park."

"Well, at least the view will be nice," she said. "Let's get this over with." She finished dressing and went to the front door, turning to Seth, who was behind her a few feet.

"Come on," she said. "Let's get moving." She opened the apartment door and walked out, not waiting for him.

Seth started to get angry, but then focused on her beautiful form walking to the sidewalk, her shapely hips swaying. She was worth it most of the time. *Almost.*

7

Frank and Jane Call

Robbie moved his stuff up into the master bedroom.

"What time are the others getting here?" Morgan asked.

"Any time now," he said. "You moving your stuff into that back bedroom?"

"I dumped it in there," she said. "Don't know if I want to sleep downstairs, though."

"You don't have to decide yet," Robbie said. There was a knock on the door. He rushed out and looked over the balcony. Gil and Justin were downstairs, Justin holding the dog's leash.

"Be right down, guys," he said, rushing for the stairs. He opened the door and Killer growled at him.

"Friend," Justin said. "Crouch and hold your hand out to him."

Robbie looked at his massive head, then glanced at Justin. "You sure?"

"Yeah," he said.

Robbie crouched and stretched his hand out slowly, Killer stretching out, his hot breath hitting him. Then he licked Robbie's hand and his tail started wagging. Robbie petted his head and Killer got closer, resting his head on Robbie's knee.

"He's in love already," Justin said, laughing. "This dog is such an attention whore once he knows you."

"Whose CRV?" Gil asked, walking in with his Winchester.

"Morgan," Robbie said. "My neighbor, remember?"

"Oh, that cute blonde?" Justin asked.

"Yeah," Robbie said. "She was left all alone there, so I said she could come here."

"Well, it'll improve the scenery quite a bit, dude," Gil said. "She's hot."

"It's crazy out there," Justin said. "We saw a lot of military around. They were pointing guns at looters, getting them lined up against buildings, and really knocking them around."

"National Guard?" Robbie asked.

"I'm pretty sure," Gil said. "Hope they're an improvement. I sensed a lot of fear out there."

"I heard gunshots," Justin said. "On the way back from my brother's house. Automatic fire. Don't think it was gang-bangers. I think it was military. I don't like this one bit."

"Call your girlfriend down here," Gil said, "so we can introduce the dog to her."

"She's not my girlfriend," Robbie said.

"Not yet, anyway," Justin said, smiling. Robbie rolled his eyes.

"Be nice," he said.

"Always," Justin said, smile on his face.

"Morgan," Robbie called out.

"Coming," she said, heading down the stairs. Killer growled.

"It's okay, boy," Justin said.

"Hi there," Morgan said, flashing an embarrassed smile. "His name is really *Killer?*"

"Yeah," Justin said. "Squat down and hold your hand out."

Morgan did that. The dog took to her quicker than he did to Robbie, licking her hand as he wagged his tail vigorously.

"He likes women more than men," Justin said. "He'll probably stick to you like glue. Hope you don't mind."

"I think he's great," Morgan said as she petted his massive head. "He looks so strong."

"Morgan, this is Gil and Justin," Robbie said. "Guys, this is Morgan."

"I've seen you back at the apartment, but we never met," Gil said, reaching out to shake hands. "Glad to meet you. Welcome."

Justin came inside and took Killer off his leash, then reached out and shook hands with Morgan. "Good to meet you."

"Thanks, good to meet you guys too," she said.

"Hear anything from Steve?" Robbie asked.

"Yeah, he'll be along," Gil said. "His uncle offered him a couple of guns. He's swinging by there to pick them up."

"Good," Robbie said. "Wish we had more ammo for your gun, Gil."

"Me too, believe me," Gil said.

"Morgan brought a handgun," Robbie said.

"What kind?" Gil asked.

"It's just a .38 special revolver," she said, "and one box of ammo, but I'm a decent shot."

"Let's go upstairs," Robbie said.

They went up and sat on the couches in the living room. Morgan was the center of attention. Killer got on the couch next to her and tried to sit on her lap.

"Sorry, boy, you're too heavy for that," she said, pushing him off. He curled up next to her and set his head in her lap. "That's better." She stroked his head, his eyes turning back towards her face.

"He's in love," Justin said.

"Don't blame him," Gil said.

She shot him an embarrassed smile.

"Yeah, the view is definitely better in here," Justin said. "Nice to have a woman around."

"Don't bug her, guys," Robbie said.

She got up. "Maybe I'll get some food going. I'm a good cook."

"Sure, go for it," Robbie said.

"There's a lot of meat in the freezer downstairs," she said. "I'll go check it out."

Robbie nodded, and then his phone rang. He looked at the number and put it to his ear.

"Mom?" he asked. "Thank God."

"Yes, honey, it's me. We're all right."

"Where are you guys?"

"We can't tell you on the phone. I'll explain it to you later. We are north east of where you are. We're in a safe place."

"All right, I understand, mom," Robbie said.

"We need to warn you about something…"

There was a pause, and whispering.

"Robbie, you're at our house?" she asked.

"Yes, Mom. I'm sorry," Robbie said. "We had to leave the apartment."

"Oh, honey, I'm not upset that you're there," she said. "I'm relieved. You don't know how worried I've been about you."

There was more hushed murmuring in the background.

"Robbie, your father wants to talk to you," she said. "Don't worry, he's glad you're there too."

"All right, mom."

"Hi, son," his father said. "Are you safe?"

"Hi, dad. Yeah, I think we're safer here. Some of my friends are with me. Hope that's okay."

"I can see them on the video," his dad said. "That's fine. Do you trust all of them?"

"Yes, of course, dad. You've met a couple of them."

"How many do you have there?"

"Three," Robbie said.

"What's been going on around there?"

"Bad stuff. A gang attacked my apartment complex yesterday. I got out with Steve and Gil. We didn't know where else to go, so we came over here."

"Anybody get hurt?"

"No. Gil had his hunting rifle. The gang tried to stop us from driving off, but when he pointed the gun at them, they got out of the way."

"Good."

"There were some problems here, too. Some thugs attacked the front unit yesterday. Rick and Diane got away, but the gang ransacked the place. Then they tried to get into the middle unit. Nobody was home, but they couldn't get the door open. We had our cars in the driveway blocking your unit. The way we parked, you can barely get past in the front. They tried to come around the back. I think one of them broke his shoulder trying to break in the back garage door. Nice job with that 4 X 4, by the way."

Robbie's dad snickered. "Good, glad it held."

"There's one bad thing. Rick and Diane were killed, on their way to the 405. The police came over this morning and told us about it. They were followed by one of the people who attacked them at the condo."

"No, really? God, sorry to hear that."

"I feel bad about it," Robbie said, "not that we could do anything."

"Watch yourselves, in case they come back, son."

"I know. We'll hang out here for a while, if that's all right with you. My job is shut down for now."

"How many guns do you guys have?"

"Gil has his 30-30 lever gun, but he's only got about fifteen rounds of ammo."

"All right. Get a piece of paper and a pencil."

"Just a sec," Robbie said. He put down the phone, and left for a moment, then came back into the living room. "OK, got it."

"Here's the combo to the gun safe. It's in the closet in the master, behind some clothes. Combo is left 35 right 12 left 8."

"Got it. What's in there?"

"Another 30-30 and about two hundred rounds of ammo, plus two Weatherby bolt action hunting rifles with scopes and about twenty rounds of ammo for each, a couple of hand guns, and a double barrel shot gun with about fifty shells. Not sure how much pistol ammo there is in there…I took a lot of it when we left."

"Thanks, dad. We'll hang out and protect your place," Robbie said.

"I'm not worried about the condo. Protect yourself, son."

"Where are you guys? When are you coming home?"

"We're in another state to the east. We got out of California just before they got it locked down. I don't know when we're coming home. It may be a while."

"I wish I was out of here too. I've been hearing bad stories about the National Guard."

"Seen any tanks around town?"

"I've seen them on the freeway, but they were all going south."

"All right, Robbie, you take care of yourself. I love you. I'll give you back to mom."

"Love you too, dad," Robbie said. He waited for his mom to get back on the line.

"Robbie, there's quite a bit of food in the deep freeze," she said. "Use it."

"OK, mom. We'll do that. We brought quite a bit of food with us too. We're OK for a week or so just on that."

"All right, honey. Be careful. Avoid the soldiers if you can."

"I'll try, mom. I love you."

"Love you too Robbie," she said. "We'll be in touch."

"Bye." Robbie ended the call, wiping tears from his eyes.

"That your mom?" Justin asked.

"And my dad," Robbie said.

"What's on the piece of paper?" Justin asked.

Robbie smiled. "Combination to my dad's gun safe."

"What's in there?" Gil asked.

"Lots," Robbie said. "C'mon, let's go open her up." He got off the couch.

"I hear a car," Gil said. "Probably Steve."

Robbie rushed downstairs, opened the door and looked out. "Yeah, it's Steve," he said. The others rushed down. Morgan joined them from the garage, a flat of chicken breasts in her hands.

"Hey, dudes," Steve said, getting out with a duffel bag. He tossed it in front of the garage door and then went back to the car, taking out two rifle cases and a metal ammo box.

"Military surplus box," Gil said. "Those are nice."

"My uncle had a lot of ammo," he said as he carried weapons inside. He went back out to get his duffel bag. Robbie closed the door after he came back in.

"Morgan, Steve. Steve, Morgan."

"Wow, she's cute," Steve said.

"Watch this guy," Gil said. "He thinks he's a player."

Robbie cracked up. Morgan got a shy smile on her face and shook hands. "Nice to meet you, Steve."

"He already knows Killer?" Robbie asked.

"Yeah, met earlier today," Justin said.

"What guns did he give you?" Gil asked.

"I don't know," he said. "Two bolt-action guns. I don't know anything about them. He says there's a couple hundred rounds of ammo in this box."

"Good," Gil said. "Let's take them upstairs and have a look."

They all went up and gathered in the living room. Morgan went into the kitchen to defrost the chicken.

"What are the sleeping arrangements now?" Justin whispered.

"I offered the back bedroom to Morgan, but I don't know if she wants to be downstairs or not."

"Where are you sleeping?" Gil asked.

"I moved into the master," he said. "but we can share that bathroom and shower."

"There's a shower downstairs, too," Gil said. "I'll probably stay in the front bedroom, if that's okay. There's an air mattress in the closet, and enough room to set it up."

"Yeah, the back bedroom will sleep more than one, too, if Morgan wants company," Steve said.

"Geez," Robbie said, shaking his head as Morgan poked her head into the room. "Sorry, Morgan."

She giggled. "Don't worry about it. I can take care of myself. Trust me."

"Let's look at these guns," Gil said. He carried them to the dining room table and laid the cases out, then opened the first one and pulled out the gun.

"This isn't a rifle, it's a shotgun," Gil said. "Bolt-action sixteen gauge. Don't see these very often."

"Is that good?" Steve asked.

"I had a sixteen gauge at home," Morgan said. "They kick a little less than a twelve gauge, but they hit almost as hard. Never saw a bolt-action model though. What kind is it?"

Gil looked at the stamp. "Sears."

Robbie laughed. "Does it say *Ted Williams* on it?"

Justin and Gil laughed. Steve and Morgan just stared at him.

"Who's Ted Williams?" Steve asked.

"Spokesperson for Sears sporting goods in the 50s and 60s. Famous baseball player."

"Oh," Steve said. "I hate baseball."

"What's the other one?" Morgan asked.

Gill opened the other case and took it out. "Whoa!"

"What is it?"

"Remington .270. This is a nice gun."

"What's a .270?" Steve asked.

"It's a necked-down 30-06," Gil said. "Too bad we don't have a scope for this. It's deadly even out at 300 yards."

"Wow, really?" Steve asked. "What does *necked-down* mean?"

"The brass casing is the same size as a 30-06," Gil said. "But the neck that holds the bullet is smaller. The bullet is .22 caliber instead of .30 caliber."

"Why is that good?" Justin asked.

"It makes the bullet fly faster for a longer distance," Gil said. "This is a great sniper rifle. Remington is a great brand, too."

"Wow," Steve said. "It worth much?"

Gil looked at it. "It's pretty much standard, so not a huge amount of money. It's worth a lot more than the shotgun."

"What's he got in the ammo box?" Robbie asked.

"Let's see," Gil said. He pulled open the latch and flipped back the top.

"Two boxes of shotgun shells and a whole lot of .270 ammo," he said. "This is great. What about that gun safe?"

"Gun safe?" Morgan asked.

"Yeah," Robbie said. "Finally got to talk to my folks. My dad gave me the combo for the safe. It's in the master. Let's go."

"Your parents are okay?" Morgan asked as they walked through the bedroom door.

"Yeah," Robbie said. "They're east. Got out of California just in time. Wouldn't tell me exactly where they were over the phone."

"Wonder why?" Steve asked.

"That doesn't sound good," Gil said.

Robbie walked to the closet, slid open the door, and moved the hanging clothes out of the way, revealing the safe.

"Damn, that's a big gun safe," Morgan said.

Robbie crouched in front of it and spun the dial to the numbers, then pulled on the door handle. It opened.

"Hey, somebody turn on the overhead lights, okay?" Robbie asked. "The switch is next to the dresser there."

"Got it, dude," Steve said. He switched them on, the overhead can lights shining down from the ceiling.

"It's the mother lode," Gil said, looking over Robbie's shoulder next to Morgan.

Robbie pulled the guns out and put them on the bed. Two bolt action rifles, a double-barrel shotgun, a Winchester 30-30 lever gun, and three hand guns.

"Wow, wonder why your parents didn't take these?" Morgan asked.

"Probably afraid they'd get confiscated," Robbie said.

"What *did* they take?" Gil asked.

"I don't see the .44 mag Winchester or the Ruger .44 mag single action revolver," Robbie said.

"Same ammo for both," Gil said. "Smart, if you can handle a .44 mag pistol. Those things kick like a mule."

"Dad's pretty good with it," Robbie said. He grabbed a couple boxes of 30-30 ammo and handed them to Gil. "Here, take these."

"Excellent," Gil said. "Thanks. If we have to do any sniper shooting, those Weatherby rifles are the hot setup. The scopes sighted in?"

"Hell, I have no idea," Robbie said. "Can you tell?"

"Only by shooting them," Gil said. "I'd keep that shotgun and the 30-30 handy."

"What handguns are those?" Steve asked.

"The big one is a .45 Colt Model 1911," Morgan said. "My dad has one of those. The other two look like 9 mm to me."

"Good eye," Gil said. "One's a Smith and Wesson Military and Police model, the other is a Beretta. Nice guns. Good for carry."

"I didn't know my dad had any automatic pistols. Wonder why he didn't take them?"

"I only see one box of ammo for each," Gil said. "That might be why."

There was a bell ringing in the kitchen.

"That's the chicken defrost," Morgan said, getting up and rushing to the kitchen.

"Damn, what a babe," Steve whispered.

"Forget it," Gil said. "You see how she looks at Robbie?"

"What are you talking about?" Robbie whispered. "She's out of my league."

"No she's not, man," Justin said. "I saw it too. You like her?"

"No comment," Robbie said. Steve snickered.

"Hell, he's in love already."

"Stop it," Robbie said. "I'm gonna put these away."

"Carry one of the pistols," Gil said. "All the time. Leave out the 30-30 and the shotgun, too."

"Okay," Robbie said. "Good idea."

The sound of automatic weapons fire floated through the air, from the direction of the Galleria.

"Shit," Steve said. "I'll bet the National Guard is killing looters over there."

"We should go turn on the TV," Gil said.

Morgan ran through the door and into Robbie's arms. "What is that?" She was trembling, fear in her eyes.

"National Guard, probably," Gil said. Justin and Steve shot a smile to each other.

"It's okay," Robbie said, rubbing Morgan's back as they embraced.

"C'mon, guys, let's go watch the TV. Hopefully they'll have something about this."

They went into the living room, leaving Robbie still holding Morgan. He pulled back from her and looked into her eyes, watching the tears roll down her cheeks. He wiped them away. "It's okay, Morgan. You'll be fine."

"I'm so scared," she said, resting her head on his shoulder. "Sorry."

"No need to be sorry," Robbie said, breaking the embrace. They sat down on the bed together.

"I don't want to sleep downstairs. Can I be in here with you? We don't have to do anything."

Robbie thought about it for a second. "I don't mind," he said. "I can sleep on the floor."

"No, we can both sleep in the bed," she said. "Like I said, we don't have to do anything. I just want to be close. I feel safe with you."

"Okay." He took her back in his arms again as she softly cried.

"Thank you," she murmured.

"It's no problem," he said, heart beating harder.

"Hey, man, we're under martial law," Gil said through the door.

"Be right out," Robbie said.

"You think they'll mind?" Morgan asked.

Robbie chuckled. "No. Well, maybe Steve will mind."

"He's a little aggressive," she said. "Not my type at all. How do you know the others won't mind?"

Robbie sighed. "Let's not talk about it."

"C'mon," she said. "What?"

"They think you like me," he said.

"I do like you," she said.

"No, *like* me," Robbie said.

"Oh," she said, an embarrassed smile washing over her face.

"Sorry," he said.

"Why do they think that?"

"C'mon, let's go out there."

"Tell me," she said, holding onto his arms, looking him in the eye.

"They said it was the way you look at me." His face turned red.

She smiled softly at him. "Okay, we can go now." They got up, but she pulled him back into her arms.

"What?" he asked.

She got close to his ear and whispered. "Your friends are pretty smart." She kissed him on the cheek, then took his hand and led him out to the living room.

8

Rocketship Park

S eth and Emma walked up to the front door of the Palos Verdes house.

"Nice house," Emma said. "Matt knows this guy?"

"He doesn't know the guy who owns the place, he knows his kid," Seth said.

"Don't tell me, let me guess," Emma said. "The parents flew the coop."

"Yep," Seth said. He rang the doorbell.

"It's open," yelled somebody inside.

"Really?" Emma asked. "The way things are going lately?"

Seth shrugged and opened the door for her.

Matt rushed over. "Hey, guys, this is Jamie," he said. "Jamie, this is Seth and Emma."

"Nice to meet you two," Jamie said. He was older than the rest of the group, with red hair and a scraggly red beard. "Welcome. There's beer in the ice chest out back."

"Great, thanks," Seth said. "How do you know Matt?"

"Work," he said. "My dad owns the company."

"Well, that explains the nice digs," Seth said.

"Where did they go?" Emma asked.

"Their house in Colorado," he said. "They wanted me to go, but I talked them out of it. I agreed to watch their house instead of staying at my place."

"I would have gone," Emma said.

"Hey, Emma!"

"Kaylee!" Emma said, rushing over to the attractive Asian girl who was walking up. "How are you? Isn't this scary?"

"Yeah, it is," she said, pushing her long black hair away from her face. "Is it safe in South Redondo?"

"So far, but you can't go anywhere," Emma said.

"My dad has guns all over the house," Kaylee said. "He thinks the problems in North Torrance are gonna come down to South Torrance. He's getting ready to split, but he's not admitting it yet."

"I'm surprised he let you come out," Matt said.

"It's because of where this is," Kaylee said. "And it's straight home afterwards. He'll ground me if I don't."

There was a knock on the door.

"It's open," shouted Jamie. When everybody turned to the door, he stared at Emma. The door opened. Trevor came in with Angel. Both of them had their Winchesters.

"Guns?" Jamie asked. "Those things loaded?"

"Yeah," Trevor said. "This is Angel. I'm Trevor."

"Jamie. Nice to meet you. What kind of guns are those?"

"They're .44 mag Winchesters," he said. "Closest thing you can get to an M4 in California. Completely legal."

"Cool," Jamie said. "My dad's into guns. He left a couple of them out of the safe for me."

"Really? What are they?" Angel asked.

"Pump shotgun and a .45 Colt auto," Jamie said. "I'm pretty good with the pistol. He put me through a combat pistol shooting class last year. The instructor said I'm a natural."

"You like it?" Trevor asked.

"It's okay," Jamie said.

"We went to the combat range yesterday," Seth said. "We all have these lever guns. We're trying to learn how to handle them in a combat situation."

"For fun, or because of what's been going on around here lately?" Jamie asked.

"Both," Trevor said. "You got yours with you, Seth? You should."

"It's in the trunk," he said.

"You brought a damn gun with you?" Emma asked.

"Hell yeah," Seth said.

She looked at Kaylee, and they shook their heads. "Let's go get a drink while the boys talk."

Kaylee nodded and they took off. Seth noticed that Jamie was very interested in both of them, nervousness creeping into his mind.

"It's worse tonight," Trevor said softly. "There's a mob down at the Del Amo Mall. They're stopping cars in the street. Flashed our guns to get by. The cops were just arriving when we went through there. Guess what else?"

"What?" Seth asked.

"National Guard. I saw several Humvees arriving at the mall."

"Martial Law," Seth said. "I knew it."

"Relax, it might be better than what we're going through now," Matt said. "I just want things back to normal."

"I don't," Jamie said. "If things get back to normal, I'll have to open up the shop again. Matt, you didn't hear that."

Matt cracked up. "I don't mind a little time off. If I wasn't living at home it might bother me."

"What about your parents, Matt?" Angel asked. "You're pretty close to Lomita and Carson."

Matt laughed. "Some of those gang-bangers showed up in Carson, by my cousin's house. Started doing home invasions. Stealing everything that wasn't nailed down. You shouldn't do that to Samoans."

"Samoans? Your cousins are Samoans?" Jamie asked

"No, but some live across the street from my cousins. They're cool. I know them pretty well."

"So what happened?" Trevor asked.

"The Samoans use their garage as a den," Matt said. "Two of the girls were out there watching the TV with the door open when a couple gang members came over. They tried to take the TV. Didn't know all the men were inside the house."

"Uh oh," Angel said.

"Yeah, uh oh," Matt said.

"What'd they do?" Jamie asked.

"They took them down to Point Fermin and tossed them off the cliff."

"Oh, bullshit," Angel said.

"I don't know, man," Matt said. "I think I believe them."

"Seriously?" Seth asked.

"Yeah, man, they're nuts," Matt said.

Angel rolled his eyes. "Let's have a beer."

"Yeah, guys, go for it," Jamie said. They walked out back to the patio, which overlooked Rocket Ship Park. Kaylee and Emma were sitting out there in lounges drinking bottles of hard lemonade.

"You guys done with the gun nonsense?" Kaylee asked. She looked at Emma, who shook her head.

"These chicks are pretty high-maintenance," Matt whispered to Jamie.

"I'll bet they're worth it," Jamie said.

"Sometimes," Seth said. "Emma's been on me since we left her apartment."

"She doesn't live with her parents?" Jamie asked.

"No, she moved out last year," Seth said. "She's got roommates. That might be why she's in a bad mood."

"What happened?" Angel asked.

"Her roommates left while she was at work. Took most of the food, including some that she bought for herself. She was pissed."

"I don't blame her," Trevor said. "Not that I like to take her side on anything."

"You don't get along with Emma?" Jamie asked.

"Not really," he said. "She thinks I'm a bad influence on Seth."

Matt laughed. "Join the club. This is one of the two nights per week we're allowed to drink."

Jamie laughed. "Allowed?"

"Long story," Matt said. "Think I'll have a smoke."

Seth looked at him and laughed. "You really want to start that up?"

"No smoking and no drinking?" Jamie asked. "Why do you put up with it?"

"Look at them." Seth sighed. "It's not as bad as we're making it sound. Emma's nice most of the time."

There were gunshots in the distance.

"Was that more gunfire?" Emma asked, looking scared. She rushed over to Seth's side. "That scares me."

"Whoa, that's automatic fire," Angel said as the gunfire continued. "It's pretty far away, though."

"I'll turn on the TV," Jamie said. "They might have something on the news."

He went from the patio into the living room and turned on the large flat-screen TV.

"Holy shit," he said. "Hey, guys, check this out."

The others came in and watched the helicopter video of the Del Amo Mall.

"Geez," Seth said. "Those look like Army guys."

"Told you we saw National Guard showing up," Trevor said.

"Who are they shooting at?" Angel said. "They've got AK-47s. Never seen any gang-bangers with those."

The announcer came on.

"As you can see, we have a battle going on at the Del Amo Mall in Torrance. Several Torrance police officers were shot, and the National Guard was brought in to help. Officials are telling us that these aren't the usual gang-bangers wanting to loot. They lured the police in and started a battle using automatic weapons and advanced battle tactics."

"That isn't good," Jamie said. "Damn, look at them go. One of those National Guard guys just got hit."

"Matt, I'm scared," Kaylee said. "That's not that far from my parent's house."

"Call them," Jamie said. "See if you can spend the night up here. We don't want to be driving anywhere near that."

"You can't get home anyway," Matt said to Kaylee. "Look at that listing on the bottom of the screen. The roads to your folk's house are closed because of this, and going around it to the east is a bad idea."

"He's right," Seth said.

"Okay, I'll call," she said.

Suddenly there was breaking glass outside, and a car alarm went off.

"Crap, what's going on here?" Jamie asked. He ran out to the backyard and looked down at Rocketship Park. There were about ten gang-bangers there, breaking car windows and searching through the cars. One of them looked up and saw Jamie, then pointed. He ducked down, and a pistol shot rang out, hitting the wood fence.

"Somebody shooting at you?" Trevor asked, running out with his rifle.

"Go inside," Jamie said in a panic. "I'm calling the cops."

"Yeah, like they'll be showing up anytime soon," Angel said. He looked at Trevor. He nodded back, and they grabbed their rifles.

"You want to shoot at them from here?" Angel asked.

"No, combat style, out there. We don't want them to know the fire came from here, or they'll bring a mess of cretins back here later."

"Matt, you got your gun?" Trevor asked.

"No, man, it's at home," he shouted.

"Pussy," Trevor said.

"Stuff it," Matt replied.

"You take the shotgun," Jamie said. "I'll take the Colt auto."

"I'm getting my gun out of the trunk," Seth said.

"No!" Emma said.

Seth ignored her and ran out the front door with the others, stopping at his trunk.

"Loaded?" Trevor asked.

"Yeah," Seth said.

"Okay, guys, remember what we learned at the combat range," Trevor said.

"And shoot to kill," Jamie said, next to them, pistol in his hand. "We can see the park when we get around that corner there. Lots of cover to hide behind. Be careful."

They rushed down, getting into planter boxes and behind trees as the gang bangers continued breaking into cars. They heard a scream, and saw a pre-teen girl being dragged into the park by her long hair.

"No frigging way," Trevor said, aiming and firing, the loud blast from the .44 mag shocking the gang bangers. He hit the one dragging the girl dead center in the chest. The girl broke free and ran, one of the gang bangers taking aim at her with a pistol. Seth shot him before he could fire, and then all of the boys were firing at the gang-bangers, hitting several before they could get to cover.

"We're gonna kill you guys," one of them shouted.

"Wanna bet?" Trevor yelled, rushing to another position. He could see several of them behind some playground equipment, and fired three times, killing two of them. Meanwhile Jamie ran to the other side of the park, rolling into the grass and firing from prone position, killing three more gang-bangers before they knew what hit them. The last two panicked and ran for their car. Matt took out one of them with the shotgun. The other one got behind the wheel, Angel hitting him in the head before he could take off. Then there was silence.

"Damn fine shooting, boys," Jamie said.

"Hell, you're pretty good with that pistol, man," Matt said.

"We better check them," Trevor said. "Stop their clocks if they're still alive, before they can call their friends."

"Isn't that murder?" Angel asked.

"No," Jamie said. "This is a war. C'mon."

They rushed to the park and checked. All of the gang-bangers were dead, so they went back into the house.

"Thank God," Emma said, rushing to Seth, throwing her arms around him.

Kaylee rushed to Matt as he set down the shotgun. "That was crazy," she said. "We could see a lot of it from the backyard."

"Yeah, you guys are actually good," Emma said.

"Hey, look, is that a tank?" Angel asked, watching the TV. It was still following the attack at the mall.

"Yeah, but it's an old one. M-60," Trevor said.

"The National Guard has moved in heavier vehicles after killing all of the attackers. They plan on using that area as a command post to protect this part of Torrance. The following roads remain closed. Hawthorne Boulevard, Sepulveda all the way to Western, Crenshaw, Prairie, Del Amo, Carson, Torrance Boulevard, 235th street, Anza, Cabrillo, Arlington, Lomita Boulevard, and PCH between Anza and Western. Police aren't saying how long these roads will be closed."

"Damn," Matt said. "You call your dad yet?"

"He called me, and told me to stay in Palos Verdes," Kaylee said. "I have an uncle who lives up here, but dad said I can stay with you instead if I want to. As long as I stay up here and off the roads."

"You're kidding," Matt said. "Doesn't sound like him. Cool."

"You're all welcome to stay here," Jamie said.

"Yeah, I can't get home either," Emma said. "All the routes are blocked."

The newsreader continued. *"In other news, police are investigating two suspected gang members they found at the bottom of the cliff at Point Fermin in San Pedro. They were badly beaten before they fell off the cliff."*

Angel shot Matt a glance.

Matt laughed. "Told you, man."

***

Sid sat on the ridge, watching the road in both directions. It was dark. He hadn't seen any cars for a while. A flashlight beam approached.

"Sid?"

"Yvonne," Sid said. "I thought you were staying down there."

She sat next to him, set down her rifle, and turned off the flashlight. "Couldn't sleep. How's it going up here?"

"Boring as hell," Sid said. "Nobody's been on the road for a while."

"That's a good thing, right?"

"Yeah," he said. "Getting close to 3:00 am. Did you sleep at all?"

"A little," she said. "I'm scared."

"Yeah, small wonder," Sid said.

"You really think we're going to get hit, don't you?"

"Yeah," he said. "Unless the Army comes in here and blocks off this whole area."

"Should we leave?" she asked. "I know you offered to stay, but I don't want to die for any of these people."

"I don't think it's going to be all that much safer anywhere else, frankly," he said. "This place is fairly easy to defend, at least. If they just send in a truckload, we'll probably win."

"Until they send a larger group later," Yvonne said. "If we do get attacked and we're losing, you have any plans?"

"You know me too well," he said. "Yeah, there's fire roads back here that our Jeep could handle with no problem, and we could get to them from the back of the park."

"You tell anybody?"

"No," he said. "Realistically, if we're in the middle of a gun battle, we might be too pinned down to drive out of here. And besides, most people here don't have off-road vehicles. If they all knew about it, they'd clog it up for the few who do."

"Oh," she said. "That's not making me feel any better."

"Crap, look," Sid said. "Convoy." He pointed to the row of canvas-backed troop transport trucks, pulled his phone out, and hit Sam's contact. It rang a couple of times.

"Sid?" Sam asked.

"Yeah, convoy coming down the road."

"Bad guys?"

"Looks like it. I'll call back if they stop at the gate. I can see it from where we are."

"Okay, I'll call the CHP."

"Good, thanks," Sid said. He ended the call.

"I really don't like this," Yvonne said.

"I know, sweetie. First three trucks past the gate without even slowing down."

"How many did you count?"

"Twelve," he said. "Four more past it."

"Please, please go past," Yvonne whispered as she watched.

"Good, that's it. None of them stopped."

"Thank God," Yvonne said.

"Gotta call Sam," Sid said. He hit his contact again.

"Sid?"

"Yeah, they went past. Dodged that one."

"Got CHP," Sam said. "I didn't like what they told me."

"Uh oh."

Yvonne looked at Sid, fear in her eyes.

"He said they expect more to come through this way, because of the pressure directly south of San Diego."

"Dammit," Sid said. "They planning to do anything about it?"

"Stretched too thin to stop them at the source, so they're counting on catching them in either Jamul or Otay Lake."

"That seems really stupid to me," Sid said.

"It's all about San Diego," Sam said. "If the bad guys continue north, it's not their problem."

"It's not the *people* in San Diego, I suspect," Sid said. "It's the military installations there."

"Yeah," Sam said. "I'm going back to bed. You gonna stay there? You don't have to."

"Might as well," he said. "Until light. I'll sleep then."

"You're a better man than I," Sam said. "Thanks."

Sid ended the call.

"What was the *uh oh* for?" Yvonne asked.

"We can expect more enemy traffic. The authorities aren't going to stop it at the border for now. They'll concentrate on the two places that lead into San Diego."

"Oh no," Yvonne said. "That's not what I wanted to hear."

"We've got to think about this," Sid said. "Decide if we stay and fortify or slip away."

"You really going to stay here until it's light?"

Sid laughed. "That's only about an hour and a half, sweetie."

"Oh," she said. "You're right."

"Vehicles," Sid said. "Dammit, those are military."

"Gonna call Sam?"

"I know he's not fast asleep. I'll call him if they stop at the gate."

"Are those guns they have mounted on the backs?"

"Yeah," Sid said. "I can't believe the CHP. Why would they want to leave the back door open down there?"

"Maybe they want problems," Yvonne said.

"First one went by the gate," Sid said. "Another two coming, though."

"You don't think they want a few of them to slip north just so they can use it to declare martial law, do you?" Yvonne asked.

Sid chuckled. "Now you're thinking like me. I hope not."

"They go by?"

"Oh, yeah," Sid said. "Sorry."

"You think they might be doing something like that?" Yvonne asked.

"Doesn't make sense to me," Sid said. "They've never had a problem coming up with a lie to justify whatever the hell they want to do. Why put people at risk when they could just lie?"

Yvonne laughed. "Hell, you're even more cynical than I am."

"More of those vehicles," Sid said. "Dammit, what a frigging parade. Something's going on."

Yvonne looked at him again, then at the road.

"First two went by," Sid said.

"Good," Yvonne said.

"Dammit, the last one stopped by the gate," Sid said, his heart pounding. He took out his phone and called Sam.

"Military vehicle just stopped at the gate," Sid said.

"What is it?"

"Vehicle similar to a Humvee, but not American. Get ready. They have a machine gun mounted to the back."

{ 9 }

Crossbow

Sam picked up his phone, frantically calling the able-bodied men in the park. Clem, John, Harry, and several others. Sid was already in play, on the side of the hill with his rifle. "He'll take out the driver in a hurry, because he'll see them first from his vantage point," Sam said to himself. The fear of problems with PTSD crept into his mind, his memories of being a Navy Seal making his heart pound. *Don't be scared, and don't forget your training.*

"Get them all?" Connie asked, checking her shotgun.

"Yeah, they're on the way up here," Sam said. "Call the CHP guys, okay? The number is by the phone."

"Will do," she said, watching him load his M4. "Be careful."

He ran out the door and took up a position just outside the main gate, behind some boulders. Clem, John, and Harry ran over and took positions around him, all of them aiming their rifles down the road.

Sid and Yvonne watched from the hillside.

"See them yet?" Yvonne asked. She checked her rifle, and scanned down from their high place.

"They have to break through the gate," Sid said. "Can't see it from here. It's got a big lock on it. They might have a little trouble."

"They could shoot it off with that gun, right?"

"They think they're going to surprise us, so they'll only do that as a last resort."

"What if they leave their vehicle and walk up?"

Sid chuckled. "If they do that, they leave their big gun behind."

"Oh," she said. "Duh."

Sid was quiet for a moment. "Actually, you got me thinking."

"What?" she asked.

"If they know we're here because of the last attack, they'll break through the gate. If they don't, they'll come on foot. They'll probably leave somebody at their vehicle. If we waste some of them on foot, we need to nail the survivors too. Blow their vehicle off the road."

"Oh," Yvonne said, watching him take his phone out of his pocket.

"Watch while I call Sam."

She nodded.

Sid hit Sam's contact and put the phone to his ear.

"You see them?" Sam asked.

"No, but I thought about something. If these guys don't know about the prior attack, they'll send a man or two in on foot."

"Crap, you're right," Sam said. "I'm gonna grab my crossbow. Take them that way if I can."

"You do that. If you end up shooting men on foot, we should chase that vehicle and take it out. We don't need them to tell others about us."

"They might call it in anyway," Sam said.

"They might. If so, at least we've got a machine gun."

"Won't they shoot us with it if we chase them?"

"If they left more than one man at the car, then yeah," Sid said. "Just be careful, and play it by ear. I know your history."

"That was a long time ago," Sam said, his breath coming hard.

"Something wrong?"

"I just ran to the house and ran back here with the crossbow."

"Good. If they knew we were here, they would've broken through the gate and driven in by now. Stay sharp."

"You too," Sid said. He slipped his phone back in his pocket and aimed the rifle, then looked over at Yvonne.

"What?" she asked.

"If we see men coming on foot instead of in the vehicle, don't shoot them right away. Let's give Sam a chance to get them with the crossbow."

"Okay," she said. They watched for another five minutes.

"They're on foot," Sid said. "Or they're sawing that damn lock with a hack saw."

They watched another few minutes, then Yvonne touched Sid's arm.

"Look, two men, side by side, coming down the access road. See them?"

"Yeah," Sid said. "Another one coming against the other side of the road, below the shoulder. Good."

"Why good?"

"Because that vehicle probably only holds four men. Somebody's in it by themselves."

"Wow," Yvonne said. "Sam just took the lone guy out, see that?"

"Yeah, that was a nice shot. Wish we had more than one bow."

An arrow flew, hitting one of the two men on the other side of the road just as they got to the front gate. The other one looked at him in shock, and then an arrow hit him square in the chest.

"How did he do that so fast?" Yvonne asked.

"Good question," Sid said. "He *was* a Navy Seal, but maybe one of the other guys has a bow too."

"Maybe," she said. "Sam's in his Jeep with Clem and Harry. John is in the back," Yvonne said. "Won't that other vehicle hear them coming?"

"Possible," Sid said. His phone rang. "It's John." He answered.

"Sid, think you can hit that vehicle on the highway if it tries to escape?"

"I can hit it, but I don't know if I can stop it," Sid said. "Why?"

"Even if we stop a couple hundred yards from the gate and walk to it, there's a good chance we'll be heard. Quiet out here."

"Okay, I'll get myself into position with Yvonne. She's a damn good long shooter too."

"Thanks," John said.

"Somebody else have a crossbow?"

John laughed. "Clem, and it wasn't a crossbow, it was his hunting bow. I didn't know he was so good with it."

"Okay, be careful," Sid said. He ended the call and looked at Yvonne. "C'mon, let's get into position to hit that vehicle on the road if it tries to run."

Yvonne nodded and followed him over, finding herself a good place to shoot prone. Sid got next to her.

"If we see it, we're gonna shoot until we stop it, okay?" Sid asked.

"Won't they shoot back with the machine gun?"

"They'll have a hard time seeing us, and we've got a lot of rocks to hide behind."

"Oh," Yvonne said. "Right."

They watched silently for a few minutes.

"Dammit," Sid said. "There it goes."

Yvonne fired at the front windshield, working the bolt furiously as Sid shot through the side windows.

"I nailed him," Yvonne said. "Look."

"You sure?" Sid asked as the vehicle rolled to a stop.

"Pretty sure," Yvonne said. "Easy shot."

Sid chuckled. "For you, maybe."

Yvonne chuckled. "Look, Sam's Jeep just pulled up behind." They watched as the men jumped out, guns pointed at the vehicle.

"Hope nobody else was in that thing," Yvonne said. "Can't see in the back."

"Yeah," Sid said. "Except where the machine gun is."

"Crap!" Yvonne said, firing as a man leapt to the machine gun. He got off a shot before he fell, hitting Harry.

"No!" Sid said. "Dammit."

"What should we do?" Yvonne asked.

"Stay put, in case somebody else joins the party," Sid said.

***

Robbie and Morgan sat on the couch nearest the TV, sipping beers. Gil, Steve, and Justin were on the other couch. Killer was curled up at Morgan's feet. It was almost 10:00 PM.

"You think they're coming back tonight?" Morgan asked.

"They might not, after what happened in Del Amo - Torrance took the brunt tonight," Gil said. "At least we have more firepower now if they do show up."

"What difference is that going to make?" Justin asked.

"Might save our lives," Gil said. "That dog is just as important, though. If somebody tries to sneak on the property, there's a good chance Killer will hear them."

"*Oh, yeah,*" Justin said. "Killer caught a burglar at my folks house once. Grabbed the guy, broke his ankle. Snapped it. They said the neighbors could hear his screams all the way down the street."

"My Killer did that?" Morgan asked, rubbing the dog's massive head with her bare feet. He looked up at her, squinting his eyes in pleasure.

"Any of those guys who try to hurt you probably won't live through it," Steve said. "That dog is *in love.*"

Morgan giggled.

"I want to know who those other men were," Robbie said. "The ones who were shooting at the police after the gang bangers ran away."

"You and me both, man," Gil said. "Been on and off the message boards for the last couple hours on my iPad. Rumor has it that those folks have been instigating the problems with the gangs."

"Lots of crazy garbage on the internet," Justin said. "You know that."

"Sometimes they're right," Gil said.

"Who are they saying these people are?" Morgan asked.

"Mixture of Islamic fighters and the Venezuelan Army," Gil said. "Well trained and equipped."

"Oh, horse shit," Justin said.

"I saw those stories too," Steve said. "I believe it. They had AK-47s tonight. Saw that on TV, remember? Gang-bangers don't have those."

"He's right," Robbie said. "Most of the gang bangers I've seen on TV have only had pistols and shotguns."

"Some of them didn't even have that," Gil said. "Remember when we left your apartment? It just took a shot over their heads to make them run away."

"What if the guys with AK-47s show up here?" Morgan asked, looking at Robbie, wide eyed with fear.

"Don't worry, it's pretty unlikely," Robbie said. "There's not much here. They'll only go after targets that will get them something."

"Yeah, Robbie's right about that," Gil said. "I'm gonna go get some shut-eye while things are calm."

"I set up an air mattress in there," Justin said. "Be down pretty soon."

"I'll take that back bedroom," Steve said.

"Take one of the guns down there with you," Robbie said. "The shotgun. You've fired a double-barrel before, right?"

"Yeah," Steve said as he left, grabbing the shotgun. Justin stayed upstairs.

"You don't look so good," Robbie said.

"I'm afraid we're going to bring something onto ourselves with all the guns," he said.

"We'll be okay," Robbie said. "Nobody knows we have them other than those guys that were at our apartment, and they don't know where we are."

"Wrong," Justin said. "The guys who we shot the other night, remember?"

"I think all of them are dead," Robbie said.

"How do you know that?"

Robbie sighed. "I don't for certain, but with the dog and the guns, if they do show up we have a good chance of taking them out."

"What if they light the condo on fire?" Justin asked.

Robbie looked over at him as Morgan put her hand on his thigh. "Will you knock it off?"

"No," Justin said. "What would happen?"

"The fire alarm would go off, and if there's flames in here the fire sprinklers will go off. Meanwhile we'll go out there and blow them away. So relax. Go get some sleep."

Justin was quiet for a moment.

"You don't think they'll really come back, do you?" Morgan asked.

"I doubt it," Robbie said. "Don't worry about it, okay?"

"Can't help it," she said, getting closer to him.

"Sorry," Justin said.

"Look, we're all nervous," Robbie said. "We'll just have to deal with it."

"I know," he said. "I'm going to bed. See you in the morning."

He went down stairs. Killer got up and followed him.

"He likes to fight with everybody, doesn't he?" Morgan whispered.

Robbie chuckled. "Yeah, pretty much. He's an okay guy, though."

"I know," she said. "Can we go to bed now?"

"Sure," Robbie said. He switched off the TV and they got up. "You sure you don't want me to stay out here? The couches are fine."

"No," she said as he helped her up. "I'm not kicking you out of your room, and, besides I don't want to be alone. It's too scary."

"Okay," Robbie said. They went into the bedroom and shut the door behind them.

"You can have the bathroom first," Robbie said.

"No, you go ahead," Morgan said. "It'll take me a few minutes to dig through my stuff."

"Okay," Robbie said. He got his toothbrush and his gym shorts and went into the bathroom. His heart was pounding. *What if they do show up?* He brushed his teeth, trying to push the thoughts out of his mind, but it wasn't working. *Can I protect her?* He took his clothes off and put on his gym shorts, suddenly wishing he'd brought a t-shirt in with him.

"You decent?" he asked.

"Yeah, I'll change in there," she said.

Robbie took a deep breath and came out of the bathroom, heading for the bed in a hurry. He grabbed the TV remote off the nightstand and switched it on. "Mind?"

"No, not at all," she said. "Be back in a few minutes."

Robbie rolled through the channels as Morgan puttered in the bathroom, door ajar. He got out of bed and switched off the ceiling lights, then turned on her bedside table lamp and hurried back into bed. Nothing much on local TV. They were still running the video from the mall over and over. He went to CNN. They were talking about rumors that Texas would leave the Union. *What?*

The bathroom door opened, and Morgan walked out in a long t-shirt with a picture of Tweety on the front. She tossed her dirty clothes on the floor, then turned to the TV and brushed her hair a few more strokes, the t-shirt lifting a little too high. Robbie tried not to look.

"Anything on?" she asked.

"Nothing but rehash of the mall video on the local channels. This discussion is about Texas."

"There's trouble there too, I heard," she said, turning towards him, setting the brush down on the dresser. She climbed into bed, watching him as he tried to keep his eyes off her. "Don't be nervous, I don't bite."

"Sorry," he said.

"Are you afraid of me?" she asked.

"No," he said quickly.

She rolled onto her side facing him, studying his eyes. "You are a little. It's okay."

Robbie looked at her soft, pretty face, her eyes misty. "I'm fine, Morgan. Sure you're okay?"

She reached out and petted the side of his face. "Think I'll turn off the light." She turned and reached for the light switch, shutting it off, then came back down on her side facing away from him.

"Good night," Robbie said.

"Why are you so far away?"

"I'm right here," he said.

"I'd feel better if you were closer. We can spoon, can't we?"

Robbie moaned. "If we do that, I might…you know."

She giggled. "I'd be disappointed if you didn't react at least a little bit. It's natural. Don't worry about it." She scooted backwards until she was against him. "See, it's not so bad."

"Easy for you to say," he said. "When you react at least you can hide it."

She giggled again. "You're so funny. Don't worry about it. I feel safe like this."

"Good," Robbie said softly.

"You aren't reacting anyway," she said. "I'd feel it."

"I'm trying really hard not to," he said.

She laughed. "What, are you thinking of dead puppies and grandma?"

They both chuckled, the movement of them against each other more than Robbie could take.

"Well finally," she said. "I was starting to feel bad." She reached for his arm and pulled it over herself, moving tighter against him.

"You're not making it any easier."

"Sorry." She chuckled again, her body shaking against him.

Robbie's heart was racing. "You're enjoying this, aren't you?"

"Yes," she said. "Sorry if I'm making you uncomfortable." Her hand came up and caressed his arm, still draped over her. "Thank you so much for bringing me here."

"No problem," he said.

"What if we have to leave? Will you take me with you?" Her body shook slightly.

"Are you crying?" Robbie asked.

"Sorry," she said.

He moved his hand up to pet her hair. "Of course you can come with us."

"I don't want to be a burden on you guys."

"Why do you think you're a burden?" Robbie asked.

"I don't know," she said. "I guess because I'm somebody else you have to protect."

"We'll protect each other," Robbie said. "Don't worry. Try to get some sleep."

"What if things get better? Will you leave me behind then?"

Robbie chuckled. "You really have a bad opinion of yourself, don't you?"

"Sometimes," she said.

"I like you," Robbie said. "Can't you tell?"

"All guys react when they're up against a girl," she said.

"I wasn't talking about *that*," Robbie said. "You're nice and you're fun to talk to and you're beautiful. We're only just getting to know each other, but I like you a lot so far. I *don't* want you to leave, no matter what happens. Okay?"

"You haven't tried anything," she said.

"Give it time. Trust me, I'm interested."

"Maybe a little more interested now," she said, pushing back against him, moving her hips around.

"That's not fair." Robbie chuckled. "Go to sleep. Okay?"

"Okay," she said.

The closeness was helping Robbie as much as it helped Morgan. They both drifted off. Every so often Robbie would stir, feeling the warm body moving next to him. He'd had girlfriends before, but this was different. Strange and exciting and scary all at once.

The sun came through the window, waking Robbie.

"You're awake," Morgan said. He was on his back. She moved closer, resting herself against his side, her arm over him. "I haven't slept that well in a couple weeks."

Robbie turned to her, their faces only inches apart as they studied each other. Then he realized that her nightgown was off.

"I know, sorry," she said. "I got sweaty in the middle of the night. Hope you don't mind."

"I don't mind," Robbie said. There it was again. He felt himself. She looked at him with a knowing smile.

"Feels like morning." She giggled and moved her leg over his torso.

"You really know how to torture a guy, don't you?"

She kissed him, just lightly, then climbed out of bed, careful to keep her back to him as she pulled her nightgown back over her head. "I'll cook breakfast. Pancakes okay?"

"You're just full of surprises," Robbie said.

She came back over, her face serious as she bent down to him and kissed him, this time with passion.

"What was that for?" Robbie asked as she pulled away.

"Partly a thank you," she said. Then she got a sly smile on her face. "Partly to let you know I like you. A lot."

She turned and went to her bag, pulled out some clothes, and went into the bathroom to change. Then she slipped out of the bedroom. Robbie laid there, mind racing.

{ 10 }

Paseo Del Mar

"Harry!" Sam shouted in the darkness.

"He's hit in the thigh," Clem shouted. "Looks like a big flesh wound, but I'll put my belt around it so he doesn't bleed too much."

"Yeah," Sam said. "Do that. John, help him, okay? I'll check this vehicle out. Make sure nobody else is alive inside."

"Got it," John said.

"Damn, this hurts," Harry said.

"It's going to take all three of us to get him into the back of your Jeep," Clem yelled.

"No problem," Sam said. "Vehicle's clean. It's a frigging GAZ Tigr."

"What's that?" John asked.

"Russian version of a Humvee," Clem said. "Read about them."

"Who wants to drive it back?" Sam asked.

"I will," Clem said. "Let's get Harry taken care of now, though."

Sam rushed over and they wrestled the big man into the back of the Jeep.

"Damn, Harry, how much do you eat?" Clem said.

"Shut up," Harry said, laughing. "Ouch."

Sam got into the driver's seat of the Jeep. Clem rushed over to the Tigr with John. They drove to the access road. Sam stopped after they got off the highway and motioned for Clem to pull next to him.

"You gonna lock the gate back up?" Clem asked from the driver's seat of the Tigr.

"No. John, call 911 okay?"

"I don't need no damn ambulance," Harry shouted from the back of the Jeep. "Let Dr. Grace look at me when we get back."

"You sure?" Sam asked.

"Yeah," Harry said. "Lock the gate."

Sam nodded and jumped out of the Jeep, running to the gate to close and lock it. He was back in the driver's seat in a few seconds, racing up the road with the Tigr behind him. They pulled inside the park and stopped next to the office.

"Sam!" Connie shouted as she ran out to meet them. "Thank God."

"Call Dr. Grace," he said. "Harry got shot."

"Oh no," Connie said. She rushed into the office to look up his number.

"Where's Harry?" Nancy asked as she hurried over.

"He got shot," Clem said.

"No!" she said, rushing to the Jeep.

"Don't worry, woman, I'm gonna be okay," Harry said. After a delay that felt longer than it was, the retired doctor arrived.

"Thanks, Dr. Grace," Nancy said.

He nodded and rushed over to the back of the Jeep, setting his black bag down next to Harry. He pulled out scissors.

"You're not gonna cut my damn jeans, are you?" Harry asked.

"Yeah, I am," he said. "Relax. If this looks even a little dicey, I'm calling 911. Oh, and by the way, you're gonna need pain meds either way."

"You can still prescribe, right?"

Dr. Grace sighed. "Yeah, but I try to avoid it. I'm supposed to be retired, remember?"

"I know, Doc. Sorry."

"Don't worry about it," he said as he cut open the jeans. He pulled out a small flashlight and took a close look. "You're lucky. We can probably just clean up the wound and bandage it. No square dancing tonight, though."

Harry cracked up. "Good excuse. Nancy won't like it."

"I heard that, you old fart," Nancy said from behind Dr. Grace.

Harry laughed hard.

"Hold still, dammit," Dr. Grace said. Then he stuck his head out of the back of the Jeep. "Hey, Connie, you guys have a stretcher around here?"

"Yeah," Connie said. "I'll round up some of the men and bring it over. Where do you want to put him?"

"One of the clubhouse tables would be good," Dr. Grace said.

"What are you gonna do to him?" Nancy asked.

"Not much, but I want to see the other side of this. I'll have to roll him on his side. Can't do it back here."

"Here they are," Connie said.

Several of the men held the stretcher, as they helped roll Harry onto it.

"Ouch!" Harry shouted.

They got him loaded and rushed him to the clubhouse, putting him on the first table inside the door. Dr. Grace moved the bench away from one side. "Need more light in here."

"Okay," Connie said. She switched on the ceiling lights. "That enough?"

"Yeah," Dr. Grace said. "Help me roll him on his side."

John and Clem leapt in to help, Harry crying out, but not as loud as when the Doc started probing the wound.

"Harry!" Nancy cried, going over to him and petting his head as the Doc started to work.

"This isn't so bad," Dr. Grace said. "You'll be okay in a week or two. This is gonna sting a little." He started washing the wound.

"Ouch, shit!" Harry shouted.

"You want an infection?" Dr. Grace asked.

"No," Harry said.

"Then man up," Dr. Grace said, squeezing the bottle again, washing the wound out. Harry gritted his teeth.

***

Up on the ridge, Sid and Yvonne watched the sun come up. "Think we can go down yet?"

"Yeah," Sid said. "Our situation just got better."

"Really?" Yvonne asked. "I figured it to be worse. Won't others come to find out what happened to those guys?"

"They might, but they'll run into a hail of machine gun fire if they do," Sid said. "Maybe I ought to brush up on my archery skills. Comes in handy."

"You'll still be good," Yvonne said. "It's like riding a bicycle, right?"

"Kinda sorta," he said. They climbed down the trail. "Hope Harry's not hurt too bad."

"Me too," Yvonne said. "Nancy must be beside herself."

"Yeah," Sid said. He laughed.

"What's so funny?"

"This will get him out of square dancing tonight."

"He hates it that much?" Yvonne asked.

"Yeah," Sid said. "Maybe I ought to get myself shot."

"You'd better not," she said.

He chuckled. "Oh, don't worry. I usually have a good time after those dances."

"Shut up," Yvonne said. She punched him in the shoulder.

"Sid," Sam said, walking up. "Yvonne. Nice shooting, you two."

"Yvonne hit the driver through the windshield," Sid said. "Beautiful shot."

"Yeah, tagged him right in the head, too," Clem said as he walked up. "Had to wipe brains out of the way before I could drive it off."

"Eeewww," Yvonne said. "Don't tell me any more."

"What'd you do with the bodies?" Sid asked

"The two by the road went down the embankment," Clem said. "They're out of sight. Got to figure out what to do with the three inside the park."

"They Islamists?" Yvonne asked.

"Looks like it," Sam said. "Reminds me of the cretins that I fought in Iraq."

"They're going to come back for them, I'll bet," Sid said. "We best be ready."

"Honey?" Connie called out from the office.

"Coming," Sam said. He trotted over to her. Sid and Yvonne followed Clem into the clubhouse. Harry was on the table, the doc and Nancy standing over him.

"He gonna be okay?" Yvonne asked.

"Yeah, he'll be fine, but he needs some better pain meds than I've got. I wrote him a prescription. Need a volunteer to go get it filled."

"I'll go," Clem said.

"No," Sam said as he walked up. "I need you and John to help me set up the video cameras."

"I can go," Sid said.

"No, you've been awake all night," Yvonne said.

"I'll go," Connie said.

"I'll go with," Nancy said.

"Okay, girls, but be careful, okay?" Sam said.

"We will, honey. Remember the CHP will be here soon with the coroner."

"Oh, that's what the call was about, eh," Sid said.

"Yeah," Connie said. "We'll leave the gate open for them when we take off. They ought to be here in about ten minutes."

"Good, then they'll get the bodies out of here," Clem said. "Let's go get the work started on the video system. I'll grab John."

"Meet you out by the flag pole," Sam said.

"C'mon, Nancy," Connie said. They walked towards the Suburban parked near the back of the office. Sarah was walking up with John and Clem.

"Hey, can I go too?" Sarah asked.

"Sure," Connie said. "Glad to have you."

Sarah left John's side and hurried towards the Suburban.

"You sure it's okay for them to go into town by themselves?" John asked.

"They should be armed," Sid said.

"Connie's got her pistol," Sam said.

"Sarah's got her purse gun too," John said. "Still worries me."

"There they go," Sid said, watching the women drive off.

"You two better go get some shut-eye," Sam said.

"Yeah, c'mon, honey," Yvonne said. "I want you rested up for the square dance tonight."

"Can't we just skip to the part after?" Sid said. She gave him an exasperated look as he chuckled.

***

Emma and Seth were sleeping next to each other on the living room floor in front of the TV, it's glow lighting them. The sound was on low. Jamie was in his room. Matt and Kaylee were in a guest room. Trevor and Angel were sleeping on couches in the living room. Angel awoke with a start. He shook Trevor.

"Whaaaa?" Trevor asked.

"Hear that?" Angel asked.

"Hear what?" Then he heard it. Footsteps, car doors. "At the park. C'mon, let's take a look."

"Careful," Angel said. "Be quiet, dude."

They snuck out to the backyard and peeked over the fence. There were gang-bangers loading up the bodies, with Islamic fighters watching, AK-47s at the ready.

"Dammit," Angel whispered as he got out of sight. Trevor got down too. "Good thing we killed them all. They don't know where we came from."

"Think they're just going to leave, or will they try to find us?" Trevor asked.

"Hopefully they'll just leave."

"If they don't, think we can take them on?" Angel asked.

"I counted four Islamists and four gang-bangers. That's less than we took on earlier."

"Yeah, but none of those gang-bangers had AKs," Angel said.

"True," Trevor said.

They stayed in the backyard, listening. Suddenly there was shouting in broken English.

"Son of a bitch," Angel said, popping his head above the fence. He got back down in a panic. "Hey, man, they're pulling people out of the houses across the street from the park."

"One of them might know where we came from," Trevor said. "Better wake the others."

"Yeah, man," Angel said. They rushed inside. Trevor shook Seth. Angel ran to the bedrooms, waking Jamie and Matt. They all met in the living room with their guns.

"So what do we do?" Jamie asked.

"I say we go take them," Trevor said.

"You want us to go against Islamist fighters with AKs?" Matt asked.

"Yeah," Trevor said. "We can do it."

"What's going on?" Emma asked, reaching for the switch on a lamp.

"Don't turn that on," Trevor said. "Enemy fighters outside."

Kaylee came out. "You aren't going out there, are you?"

"You want them coming in here?" Angel asked. "They're pulling people out of houses around the park. One of them probably knows where we came from."

"Lock and load, gentlemen," Jamie said.

"Yeah, what *he* said," Trevor said. The boys loaded their guns and grabbed extra ammo, then snuck out the front door. A woman screamed, then a man yelled. There was a single gunshot, and more women screaming.

"Shit, they just shot that woman's husband," Trevor whispered as they peeked around the corner. "Now they're tearing her nightgown off."

"That ain't gonna stand," Jamie said. "C'mon."

Trevor shot first, hitting one of the Islamists who was assaulting the woman. The others opened fire, dropping two more Islamists, leaving only one, who dived under cover, firing wildly in their direction. The gang-bangers raced for two trucks and a car. Seth fired at the first truck, splattering the brains of the driver all over the inside of the cab, the two men with him screaming. Matt leveled the shotgun and fired into the cab, the blast hitting both of the other men in the face.

"Look out," Trevor said, nodding towards the Islamist, who was running at them with his AK-47. Seth, Trevor, and Angel all popped up and fired, hitting him with at least two .44 mag slugs, dropping him right away.

"That was the last of the Islamists," Trevor shouted. "Get that car and the other truck!"

All of them raced out into the open and fired, several bullets crashing through the windshield of the truck as it attempted to roll past them. It went out of control and drove onto the porch of a house.

"Get the car!" Angel shouted. He fired. Jamie ran out and emptied a clip into the side windows, but the car got away, heading around the corner before they could stop it.

"Let's go check for survivors," Jamie said.

"Yeah, and *stop their clocks*," Trevor said.

Seth looked at him and snickered.

"Careful, you guys, they might have somebody left that can shoot back," Angel said. "Stay under cover as much as possible."

"He's right," Jamie said. He ran in a crouch, pistol in two-handed combat grip as he got to the spot where two Islamists were hit. They were both dead, as was the one who had been assaulting the woman.

"This one bought it too," Seth said, poking the fourth Islamist with the barrel of his Winchester.

Several of the neighbors came out slowly, looking in all directions. One of them had a shotgun with him.

"Thanks," he said. "You saved Gretchen from being raped right out in the open."

The woman walked over, holding her torn nightgown around herself, reaching out for Trevor and kissing him on the cheek. "Thank you so much."

"You're welcome," Trevor said.

"If I were you kids I'd get the hell out of here," the old man with the shotgun said. "They know which house you came out of."

"How?" Jamie asked.

"One of your neighbors told them just before you opened up," he said.

"We might be okay," Matt said. "Only one of them escaped, in that car."

"How many were in the car?" Seth asked.

"I was pretty close," Jamie said. "Only saw the driver."

"Might have been somebody else in there, staying down," Seth said.

"That's true," Jamie said.

"I don't think we can trust that the person or persons who escaped don't know which house," Seth said. "I think we should take off before they come back."

"And go where?" Angel asked.

"Kaylee's uncle," Matt said. "He lives way on the far side of the hill."

"There's your ticket," the old man said. "You'd better scoot before they show up."

"What about you guys?" Seth asked.

"We'll be okay," the old man said. "I got more guns hidden away, and so do several of my neighbors."

"Okay, thanks," Jamie said.

The boys walked back towards the house.

"If those guys are so ready, why'd we have to save their bacon?" Angel asked.

"Same thing I was thinking," Seth said.

They walked into the house. Kaylee and Emma rushed up.

"Kaylee, call your uncle," Matt said. "We need to get out of here now."

"It's 4:00 AM," she said.

"Don't care," Matt said. "One of the gang-bangers got away, and one of the people those Islamists were terrorizing told them about this house."

"Shit," Kaylee said, rushing into the guest room to get her phone.

"You guys mind if I come along?" Jamie asked.

"Are you kidding?" Matt asked. "You'd *better* come along."

"Yeah, seriously, man," Angel said.

"Those weren't just gang-bangers out there, were they?" Emma asked.

"There were four Islamists out there," Seth told her.

"We should have grabbed their weapons," Angel said.

"Let the neighbors have them," Trevor said. "We trained on the Winchesters. That's the best thing for us at this point."

"Yeah, I think you're right about that," Seth said.

Kaylee rushed back out into the living room. "He said we could all come over."

"He's got room?" Seth asked.

Kaylee cracked up. "He's rich. Wait till you see his place."

"Yeah, been there once," Matt said. "It's got a panoramic view of the ocean. Catalina Island to the south, Santa Monica Bay to the north. It's bitchen, man."

"You guys have to behave," Kaylee said. "Watch your mouths when you're there."

"How about the guns?" Trevor asked.

"He said to bring them. He's a gun nut too. You guys will get along just fine."

Matt chuckled. "Yeah, I think that's why he likes me."

"All right, let's load 'em up," Jamie said. "Before we get company."

"Which cars?" Trevor asked.

"All of them," Jamie said. "C'mon. Which way?"

"Get on PV Drive West heading south," Kaylee said. "Take a left on Cloyden Road, then another left on Paseo Del Mar."

"Holy crap, that's a high priced area, all right," Jamie said. "What does your uncle do?"

"Import business," Kaylee said. "Korean electronics."

They were ready to go in less than ten minutes. Matt and Kaylee led the way. As they were leaving the neighborhood, automatic weapons fire opened up behind them.

"Dammit, you think that's them?" Matt asked. Kaylee looked over at him, eyes wide.

"Drive faster," she said.

"Yeah, I think you're right," Matt said, pouring on the speed. His sedan took off, the others speeding up behind him. They hit PV Drive West and sped up more, the street deserted. Then they made the two lefts, turning into the driveway of the mansion on Paseo Del Mar. The others followed them through the gate. When they were all on the huge curved driveway, a small middle-aged Korean man walked out with a remote and clicked it, the big heavy gate rolling across the driveway entrance.

"Welcome," he said as they got out of the cars.

"Thanks, Uncle Ji-Ho," Kaylee said, rushing over and hugging him. "Where's Aunt Ha-Yoon?"

"I sent back home when trouble started," he said. "She's with mother in Busan."

"Oh," Kaylee said. "There's no trouble over there?"

"Yeah, my sources said North Korea involved with the trouble here and Europe, but at least she not up in Seoul. That way too close to DMZ."

"Good," Kaylee said.

"Heard from parents?" Ji-Ho asked.

"Yeah, and I'm worried," she said. "They can't get here. All the roads are closed."

"I think there be martial law soon," Ji-Ho said. "Introduce me to friends."

Kaylee did the formal introductions, and they all went inside the mansion.

11

Cameras

C lem walked up the dusty driveway, tired from a long day.

"That's all the cameras," Sam said.

"They were easy, except that flagpole," Clem said. "Let's go to the *console* and check them out."

"Oh, you mean the clubhouse PC?" John asked. He looked at Clem and snickered.

"Yeah, yeah," Clem replied. "Hey, it was my job for years, okay?"

"What would have happened to your career if these new wireless cameras were out then?" Sam asked.

"At first it would have made things easier," Clem said. "Eventually people would've gotten wise to how easy they are to set up."

The three men walked towards the clubhouse door.

"A lot of jobs like that are going away," John said. "Wait until robotics really hits. It'll tear the country apart."

"I know," Sam said. "Though I wouldn't mind having a robot or two to help out at the park."

John snickered. "Doing what?"

"Cleaning the toilets, for instance."

"That wouldn't be bad," Clem said, "but it *will* take some jobs away."

"True," Sam said as he turned on the clubhouse lights. The PC was in the far corner of the room.

"That fresh coffee I smell?" Clem asked.

Sam turned on the PC and then looked at Clem. "Yeah, the big pot is on, but Connie made it before they left for town, so it might be a little raspy."

"I wish they'd get back," John said. "Been a while."

"Me too," Sam said. "You want to do the setup, Clem?"

"Sure," he said. The others watched as he sat down in front of the PC and opened the surveillance program. He got all the cameras connected within a couple of minutes.

"That's pretty easy," John said. "I see what you're talking about."

"Told you," Clem said. "You can cycle through the cameras every five seconds, or pick one and stay on it."

"How does the front one look?" Sam asked.

"Let's check it out," Clem said. "See the selection dialog box here?"

"Yeah," Sam said, looking at the screen. Clem clicked it and the front camera came on. There was a clear view all the way to the bend in the road. "Wow, that's great!"

"Tell me about it," Clem said. "What's next?"

"The gate alarm," John said. "Let's go get it done."

"The stuff is in the back of my jeep," Sam said. "Let's go."

They piled in and drove down to the front gate by the highway.

"Hope that cordless drill you got is enough to get through the metal," John said.

"It'll be good enough," Clem said. "No problem."

They worked on it for about twenty minutes, just as the day was starting to heat up.

"Here come the girls," John said. "Thank God."

The SUV drove through the gate and stopped. The women got out.

"Get what you needed?" Sam asked.

Connie shook her head yes. "They didn't have the pain meds, so we had to wait while a runner drove to the next town and back. That's why it took so long."

"That town felt awful locked down," Sarah said.

"Sure did," Nancy said. "How'd you do with the video system?"

"Done," Clem said. "The alarm is the last piece."

"Glad you girls are back here," John said, putting his arm around Sarah's shoulders. "I was worried sick."

"You didn't see any enemy vehicles when you were out?" Sam asked.

"Not a one," Connie said, "but people are scared to death."

"Yeah, that runner didn't really want to go," Sarah said. "Can't say that I blamed him."

"Let's go back," Nancy said. "I want to check on Harry."

"Okay," Connie said. "You coming, Sarah?"

Sarah kissed John. "Yeah, I'm coming." She hurried over to the SUV.

The men watched as they drove towards the park.

"Pull that gate closed," Clem said as he worked on the wiring.

John and Sam walked the gate shut and put the hasp down to hold it in place. Clem put the batteries in as Sam drilled holes in the thick metal. Then Clem mounted the device.

"Does this sound a buzzer down here when it goes off?" John asked.

"No, it uses a radio signal that goes to the alarm up at the park.

"How loud is it?" Sam asked.

"It's in the back of the Jeep," Clem said. "Let's try it out." He got it out and switched it on.

"Battery operated too?" John asked.

"Yep," Clem said.

"What's to stop somebody from taking the batteries out of that unit on the gate?" John asked.

"This key," Sam said, holding up a strange looking device.

"Most people don't know what these alarms are," Clem said. "It's also got a fail-safe. If somebody removes it from the gate or breaks it open, its internal backup system will send a signal. It sounds different than the normal alarm."

"Ready for me to open the gate?" Sam asked.

Clem set the remote speaker on the hood of the Jeep and then plugged his ears. "Go for it."

Sam pulled the gate open, breaking the connection on the sensor, and the speaker made an ear-splitting siren noise.

"Holy cow," John said, covering his ears. Sam laughed and closed the gate.

"How long does that go on after the gate has been opened?" John asked.

"If it stays open, three minutes, and then every five minutes until the gate is closed," Clem said. "We can adjust the volume. This is the default. We should figure out how much volume can be heard down here and adjust accordingly."

"Yeah," Sam said. "I'll take you guys up and then come back here and open the gate."

"Okay," Clem said. "I'd lock that."

"Oh, yeah," Sam said, putting the big padlock onto the hasp and closing it. "Let's go."

They jumped into the Jeep and Sam hit the gas.

Connie ran up to them as they pulled into the RV Park.

"Sam, the CHP called. They want you to call them."

"About what?" Sam asked.

"They didn't say," Connie said.

"If they find out about our machine gun, they're liable to confiscate it," John said.

"We won't let them do that," Sam said. "I'm going back down to the gate. Stand by with the remote speaker. I'll call you if I don't hear it."

"Okay," Clem said. "Connie, send a message out on the PA telling people this is a test. We don't want a panic."

John laughed. "Yeah, this sucker is loud."

Sam jumped into the Jeep and took off towards the highway gate.

"What's he doing?" Connie asked.

"We want to adjust the alarm so it can't be heard down by the gate," John said.

"Oh, I get it," Connie said. "You don't want them to know about the alarm."

"Yep," John said. "Hey, Sarah."

"Hi, sweetie," she said.

"How's Harry?" he asked.

"Better now that he's got decent pain meds," Sarah said. "Dr. Grace was in with him when we got back. Said he's gonna come through fine."

"Good, glad to hear it," John said.

The group milled around in front of the clubhouse for a few minutes.

Suddenly the alarm went off, making everybody jump.

"Shoot, I forgot to send out the PA message," Connie said, running to the office as the siren sounded.

"That thing is awful," Sarah shouted.

"Yeah, but it might save our lives," John said.

The siren stopped after a couple minutes. Connie's voice came over the PA system.

"Attention everybody. That was only a test. Everything is okay."

Clem's phone rang. He answered it.

"Yeah, Sam," he said.

"Did it go off?"

"Sure did. You hear it?"

"Nope," Sam said. "Guess we're okay. I'll lock the gate and come back up. Look around for a good place to park the Tigr, okay? Hidden but with a clear shot down the road."

"You got it," Clem said. He ended the call.

"He can't hear it down there?" John asked.

"Nope," Clem said. "He wants us to look for a place to park the Tigr. I think I know a good place."

"Let's check it out," John said. They walked down the pathway, past the office, then down a little further to a small berm next to the road, heavily wooded.

"How about this?" Clem asked. "We can shoot from here. They won't know what hit them."

"Tight squeeze," John said.

"True, but I think it'll fit. Maybe we should get out a tape measure to be sure."

"Got one in my rig," Clem said.

They walked back past the office. Connie came out onto the veranda in front of the door.

"Sam back yet?" she asked.

"Ought to be any second now," Clem said.

"Good. That CHP officer called again."

"Officer Ryan?" John asked.

"Yeah," Connie said. "He sounded worried."

"Wonderful," Clem said. "Here comes Sam now."

"Sam!" Connie shouted. "They called again. It was Officer Ryan."

"Okay, be inside in a minute."

"Thanks," she said.

"Find a good place for our new toy?" Sam asked.

"Yeah, just going to get my tape measure," Clem said. "It's a little tight."

"Good," Sam said. "I'll talk to you after I finish with the CHP."

***

"I'm bored, man," Steve said. "We've just been sitting around all day."

Robbie laughed. "You've heard all the gunshots out there. I think we should stay right here. We have everything we need. Have a beer."

"Most of what we've heard is automatic fire," Gil said. "It's the National Guard fighting those guys we saw last night on TV. Must be a hell of a lot of them."

Morgan came up the stairs. "Think I should thaw out that turkey? I know how to cook them, and the meat will last us for days."

"I'm game," Robbie said.

"Oh, *hell yeah,*" Justin said. "Damn, Robbie, you got yourself a good girlfriend."

"And the teasing begins," Gil said, laughing.

Robbie looked at Morgan and shrugged. "Sorry."

She sat next to him on the couch and put her legs up on his lap, then looked at Steve and smiled.

"You're enjoying this, aren't you?" Robbie whispered.

"As a matter of fact, I am," she said. Gil, Justin, and Steve cracked up.

"Maybe we ought to get *your* girlfriends over here," Robbie said.

"Mine took off with her parents to Idaho," Justin said. "That relationship was hanging by a thread, though. She wouldn't want to be here."

"I'm between girlfriends right now," Gil said. "As usual."

Steve was quiet, his face turning red. He looked on the verge of tears.

"What's the matter?" Robbie asked.

"Oh, nothing," he said. "It's stupid."

"What, man?" Robbie asked.

"Colleen," he said. "This luscious redhead that I work with. I was trying to get up the courage to ask her out. I waited too long."

"You have her number?" Morgan asked. "I see that look on your face. Us girls like that kind of reaction."

"Does she like you?" Justin asked.

"I don't know," Steve said. "We flirt some at work, but she keeps a certain amount of distance. Won't let it go too far. She thinks I'm a weasel."

Morgan laughed out loud. "You're no weasel," she said. "If I wasn't sweet on *someone* I'd be interested." She put her hand to her mouth. "Did I just say that?"

Everybody but Robbie and Morgan laughed.

"I'm sorry," she whispered.

"Did you really mean that?" he asked.

"Yes," she whispered.

"I think I'll take Killer out in the backyard," Justin said. "C'mon, guys, let's get some air."

The others got up and followed Justin and the dog downstairs.

"You have really nice friends," Morgan said. "You know that, right?"

"Yes, I know that," he said. "You aren't going to tire of me right away, are you?"

She looked in his eyes. "You want me, don't you?"

He looked at her, trying to find the words to say.

"Morgan," he said. "I'm not sure how…"

She put her finger on his lips. "You don't need to say anything. I can see it in your eyes. We'll go as fast or as slow as you want to."

He looked at her, the tears clouding his vision.

"You *have* had a girlfriend before, haven't you?" she asked.

"Yes," he said. "Two. One for quite a while. We had a nice time together, but very innocent. The second one was a shorter time. She hurt me a little."

"A little?"

"She used me," Robbie said. "She wasn't popular at school, but I thought she was beautiful, and she sang like an angel."

"You're a musician?"

"Kind of," Robbie said.

"How did she hurt you?"

"I was convenient. She strung me along. I knew she wasn't that into me, but I was trying to win her over. Didn't work. She finally broke it off when it was obvious that I was in love with her."

"How long ago was that?"

"Couple years," Robbie said.

"I'm not going to hurt you," Morgan said.

Robbie was quiet for a moment.

"You okay?" she asked.

"Yeah, sorry," he said. "I know you're not like that; figured it out pretty quickly. I'm just having a problem wrapping my head around it, that's all."

"What do you mean?"

"Hell, you look like a model. I've seen the guys you've had around. You're out of my league."

"Oh, that again," she said. "Trust me, you are exactly in my league. You just don't understand what women want."

Robbie chuckled.

"Why are you laughing?" she asked. "How many beautiful women have you asked out? I'll bet it's none, because you give up before you start."

"That pretty much sums it up," he said. "You really would've gone out with me before?"

"In a heartbeat," she said. "A smart guy who can hold down a job, and is handsome too? Sounds like a good person to have babies with to me."

Robbie laughed. "We're headed to a family already?"

"Hey, it's biology," she said. "There *are* some hot women who want to screw around with the surfer guy who works at a fast food joint. They aren't the majority, and they usually have self-esteem problems. Most women are looking for a partner, not somebody they have to take care of. *A mate.* You're good mate material. Big time. So maybe we ought to stop wasting time with the BS. I know you like me. It's easy to tell."

"I told you I liked you," Robbie said.

"I knew before you told me," she said. "Come downstairs with me. You're going to play the man and carry the turkey upstairs. It'll have to defrost for a day or two."

"Okay," Robbie said. He watched Morgan's legs as she lifted them off his lap and stood up. He stood next to her, then took her into his arms and kissed her, hard and passionate. It went on for almost a minute. They broke it and looked into each other's eyes.

"Now *that's* what I'm talking about," she said, her eyes dancing with his. She moved forward and started another kiss, their embrace becoming tighter, their breath coming quickly.

"My God," she said. "That works."

"Yeah," Robbie said. "That was pretty intense."

They went down the stairs together, looking at each other's face every few steps.

The back bedroom door opened when they were in the hall.

"What are you guys doing?" Steve asked.

"Taking the turkey upstairs to defrost," Robbie said. "You look happy."

"I called my friend from work, and he had Colleen's number."

"You going to call her?" Morgan asked.

"Working up the nerve now," he said.

"What is it with you guys?" Morgan asked. "Don't over-think it. Call her. Now. If you wait you *will* lose your nerve."

He shot her a sheepish look and nodded yes, then went back into his room, shutting the door.

Robbie and Morgan went into the garage and opened the chest freezer.

"Think he'll do it?" Robbie whispered.

"He's got a real case for her," Morgan said. "I can see it in his eyes when he talks about her. Have you met her?"

"I've seen her a time or two. She's pretty. Beautiful face and red hair. Looks like she just got off the boat from Ireland."

"They can have a temper, you know," Morgan said. "He's a nice guy. Most women are gonna be interested. Trust me."

Robbie reached into the freezer for the turkey. "Damn, this is a big one."

"It is," Morgan said. "I'll hold the door open for you."

They rushed the turkey upstairs together. "Where do you want it?"

"Just on the counter for now," Morgan said. "I need to fill one side of the sink with water and then soak it. The sink needs to be cleaned first. I'll call you when I need it lifted again, okay?"

"Okay," he said. "Mind if I watch you?"

"Doing this?" she asked. "No, run along. You can watch me later, at a more interesting time."

Robbie shook his head, walked into the living room, and dropped into a recliner, thinking about what just happened. *Could she?* He felt his heart quicken as the thoughts raced into his brain.

"Robbie, I'm ready for you," Morgan said lightly.

He got up and walked into the kitchen, his whole body electric, and stopped, taking in her shape as she finished filling the sink with water. She turned to him, her sweet eyes piercing his. "I'm ready for you to lift it in. Slowly!"

Robbie snapped himself out of it and picked up the ice-cold turkey, moving it into the water.

"Perfect," she said, turning to him. "Wash your hands and dry them."

"Oh, yeah," he said. "Salmonella."

Morgan smiled as he finished. "What do you want to do now?"

"Another kiss?" he asked.

"That can be arr…"

"Hey!" Steve shouted up the stairs.

"What?" Robbie asked.

"Colleen! I called her. She's trapped. We have to go get her!"

Morgan looked at Robbie and mouthed *NO*.

"Robbie, can you go with me?" Steve called.

"Robbie," Morgan said, worry in her eyes.

12

Liberty and Tyranny

Seth woke up next to Emma in one of the guest rooms. They had been up late watching the battles on TV. Ji-Ho hit it off with everybody right away, especially Trevor, due to their mutual love of guns.

"You awake already?" Emma asked. She stretched while looking at him. "Think we can go back to my place now?"

"Don't know," Seth said. He got out of bed and put his shirt and pants on. "It's been several hours since I've heard automatic weapons fire."

"I was asleep as soon as I hit the pillow," Emma said. She stood next to the bed and got dressed.

"We'll see what the TV says about road closures. If the roads are okay, we should be able to take off."

They picked up their things and went into the living room. Trevor and Ji-Ho were asleep in the recliners facing the TV, which was running softly in the background.

Matt and Kaylee came out of the hallway, Jamie and Angel following them.

"Sleep well?" Jamie asked, looking at Emma. She nodded yes while Seth shot him a glance.

"The roads open yet?" Matt asked. "Kaylee wants to go home."

"Emma too," Seth said.

"You can forget," Ji-Ho said, turning towards them as he rubbed his eyes.

"Everything is still locked up?" Matt asked.

"They start martial law today," Ji-Ho said. "Lock down, stabilize, then can go."

"How long are they saying it's gonna be?" Emma asked.

"Two day," Ji-Ho said. "Said late last night."

"Oh no," Kaylee said. "I'd better call my folks."

"Yes, you call them," Ji-Ho said. "Tell my brother you and friends fine. Can stay until safe."

Trevor stirred and woke up, startled when he saw everybody in the living room. "What time is it?"

"Only about seven," Seth said.

"Dammit," Trevor said. "I think I need to sleep a little more."

"Back bedroom open," Ji-Ho said. "Be my guest. See you later on. We talk more. I show you my guns and reloading setup."

"That would be great," Trevor said, getting off the couch. "Back here?" He walked towards the hallway.

"Yes, last room on left side," Ji-Ho said. "I go sleep for while in my room too. You kids make selves at home. Plenty food in kitchen." He got up. "Stayed up talking too long. Trevor nice kid. Glad to know."

"Thanks so much, Uncle Ji-Ho," Kaylee said.

"Glad you here," he said as he walked away. "Nice friends. I impressed." He went up the stairs next to the hall.

"What a nice guy," Seth said.

"Yes, he's my favorite uncle," Kaylee said. "His English keeps getting better too."

"I have no problem understanding him," Jamie said. "Are we sure everything is locked down?"

"Let's watch some TV and see," Seth said. He picked up the remote and turned the sound up. Everybody found a seat and watched.

"They ain't saying shit," Angel said. "They're tip-toeing too much. Wonder how many civilians they've killed so far?"

"Really?" Matt asked. "You going there?"

"You trust the state government?" Angel asked. "I don't."

"I'm somewhat inclined to agree, after the hassle of buying firearms and ammunition," Seth said. "The state only begrudgingly allows you to exercise your rights."

Jamie laughed. "I can't believe I've actually found people that agree with me, and they're just kids."

"You're only about five years older than us, man," Matt said.

"That many years makes a big difference when you're under thirty," Jamie said with a twinkle in his eye. "Anyway, I meant no offense. You guys are great, and we share the healthy fear of government."

"Let's go see if there's anything good to eat," Kaylee said to Emma.

"Okay," Emma said. They got up and walked into the kitchen.

"How do you guys contain yourselves around them?" Jamie asked.

"You're leering at them way too much, man," Seth said. "I don't like it."

"Seth," Matt said.

"C'mon, man, he's doing it to Kaylee too," Seth said.

"Hey, I don't mean anything by it," Jamie said. "You guys don't know how lucky you are."

Seth laughed. "You're a good-looking dude with a good job. Why don't you have a girlfriend...or a wife, for that matter?"

"I did," Jamie said. "Didn't work out."

"Well here's the scoop on Emma," Seth said, lowering his voice. "She's high maintenance. *Really* high maintenance. It's almost sunk us more than once. Be careful what you wish for."

"So why do you stay with her?" Jamie asked. "No offense, just wondering."

Seth sighed. "There's more good than bad," he said.

"You're locked in," Angel said. "Been with her too long. I think you ought to get out of it before you end up married."

Matt laughed.

"What's so funny, dude?" Angel asked. "You're in the same situation, only worse. I'd give a marriage between you and Kaylee about a year."

"Why do you say that?" Matt asked. "Hell, you know me better than anybody. Since grade school."

"That's why I say it," he said. "You can't keep it in your pants."

Seth chuckled. "You *are* kind of a horn dog, man."

"Both of you guys can shove it," Matt said.

"Don't worry, we've got your back," Angel said. "Forever."

"Wish I would've had friends like you guys when I was your age," Jamie said.

"Hey, they're talking about the roads," Seth said, turning the TV volume higher.

The news reader came on. *"This just in. The major roads in the South Bay remain closed as the National Guard sets up checkpoints to be used when Los Angeles County martial law goes into effect. The roads will be shut down for two to three days. Anybody who is in desperate need of food or medications is asked to call 1-555-334-6637."*

"Well there you go," Seth said. "We're stuck here for a little while."

"Kaylee's uncle won't mind," Matt said. "He likes you guys. Especially Trevor."

"I can tell, but I hate to take advantage," Jamie said.

"He's not looking at it that way," Angel said. "He's glad we're here, since his wife is gone. He's lonely, and he adores his niece."

"Yeah, he likes us being here," Matt said. "He told me last night."

"Okay, then we need to relax and take a few days," Seth said. "Not the worst thing in the world, by the way. This could be a good place to ride out the storm."

"The public is being warned that the bearing of arms in the South Bay is not allowed while martial law is in place," the news reader said. *"People caught with guns on their person or in their vehicles will be subject to arrest."*

"Dammit," Angel said. "We might have to ditch our guns before we can leave, or maybe ask Ji-Ho to keep them until things settle down."

"Sounds like it," Seth said. "They did this during Katrina. Screw them. They don't have the right."

"Might makes right," Jamie said.

"So what do you suggest?" Seth asked.

"Lie," he said. "Hide your guns as best you can and lie. And don't be afraid. They'll see it. Hide your feelings, and don't give up your guns. Ever."

"I'm starting to like this guy," Angel said.

"Yeah," Seth said. "Me too. As long as he keeps his mitts off our girlfriends."

Jamie laughed. "Don't worry, just looking. They have any friends?"

Seth laughed. "Yeah, even a couple who just love older guys."

"Lindsay would go for it," Matt said, "but let's not change the subject. What happens if we take our guns and get caught?"

"You'll get arrested and lose your guns," Jamie said. "Probably no more than that."

"At least for now," Seth said. "I've read about what happens after the military has been in control for a while."

"What happens?" Matt asked.

Seth looked him in the eye. "Extortion. Rape. Killings. Other bad stuff."

"Now you sound like Trevor," Matt said.

"He's studied this," Seth said. "Don't take it lightly. We, as citizens, need to make sure that this martial law is only in place as long as needed."

"You think California is going totalitarian?" Angel asked.

"I'm just saying we need to keep our eyes open," Seth said. "You know how governments can get."

"Listen to yourself, man," Matt said.

"No, he's right," Jamie said. "Happened before. I can tell you exactly what's going to happen."

Matt snickered. "Here comes the Libertarian pitch."

"You're a Libertarian?" Angel asked. "Me too."

"Me three, for the most part," Seth said.

"All right, all right," Matt said. "Go on, boss."

Jamie looked at them silently for a moment. "Okay. They'll get the bad guys locked down here in a hurry, and then entrench a very organized control over the population *for our own good*. People like us will start to tire of it after a while, and we'll begin to resist. The soldiers will become suspicious and target those who are giving them a hard time. They'll begin to look at themselves as different than the population at large. They'll become more and more oppressive. It's not going to end well for either side."

"You're assuming that the State and the Feds will keep martial law in place too long," Matt said.

"You're right, I am," Jamie said. "You know how the government of California is. You know how the current administration in DC is. I wish our governor had the balls that Governor Nelson does."

"Governor Nelson?" Matt asked.

"Texas, you dummy," Angel said. "Rumor has it that he's gonna take Texas out of the Union for a while."

"No way," Matt said. "They tried that once. Civil War, remember?"

"I wasn't here then," Angel said.

Jamie snickered. "Hey, I'm not saying the rumors are true, but I'd expect Nelson to stand up against the Feds to protect his people. Governor Sable? Not so much. He'd do the Administration's bidding even if it was bad for the individuals living in his state."

"You always say that," Matt said. "Why do you hate the guy so much?"

"He's a statist," Jamie said. "He thinks the state is more important than the individual. He thinks the individual serves the state, not the other way around. If left unchecked, that always leads to tyranny. That mindset changes the relationship between the people and their government."

"Cue the patriotic music," Matt said. "I know what's coming."

"Shut up," Seth said. "He's right."

Jamie smiled. "Lincoln, controversial as he was, said it best...*and that government of the people, by the people, for the people, shall not perish from the earth.* It is our responsibility to preserve our liberty. Never forget that, or we're lost."

"Lincoln was controversial?" Matt asked.

"You don't get it, do you?" Angel asked.

"I get it," Seth said. "Never trade liberty for security. The government always takes things too far. They always pursue the chance to increase control."

"Exactly," Jamie said.

"So what, do you want us to go attack the National Guard?" Matt asked.

Jamie chuckled. "Not yet. Just remember who they are, and who you are. Remember the Bill of Rights. Remember what made this country great. Don't give it up. Martial law for our current situation is probably good, but remember that it is supposed to be *temporary*. If it takes on an air of permanence, the people must rise up."

"Are you guys talking politics again?" Emma asked as she walked into the room.

"Yeah," Matt said. "Getting a little thick in here."

"It was a good discussion," Seth said. "Find anything to eat?"

"Kaylee's making pancakes. Anything else on the news about the roads?"

"Nope," Seth said. "Were gonna have to stay here for a couple of days."

"Shit," Emma said. "Oh well, maybe the pool is heated. You see the backyard? Wow."

"Yeah, this is definitely how the other half lives," Angel said.

"What are you gonna use for swimsuits?" Matt asked with a twinkle in his eye.

Seth laughed. "Yeah, that might be a problem."

"I don't think it's a problem," Matt said.

"Shut up," Emma said. She went back into the kitchen. Matt and Seth looked at each other and snickered.

***

"The Tigr's gonna fit, barely," Clem said as he let the tape measure reel itself in. "Might have to chop a few small branches so the gun can swing around easy enough."

"Yeah, that's what I was thinking," John said. "When we're doing that, somebody should be standing down the road to make sure we don't ruin the cover."

"Yeah," Clem said. "Let's get with Sam and make sure he's good with our plan. Then I'll drive the Tigr over."

They walked to the office and opened the door. Sam and Connie were sitting behind the counter, staring at each other, fright in their eyes.

"Damn, you two look like somebody crapped in your punchbowl," John said.

"Just got off the phone with the CHP," Sam said. "Our forces south of the border got overrun. They said to expect a flood of enemy traffic."

"Dammit," Clem said. "Maybe we ought to re-think this place."

"Probably too late," Connie said. "Officer Ryan said they're already on the highway in."

"Then we'd better get busy with the Tigr," Clem said. "We found a good place. Might have to chop out a few branches so we can aim the gun."

Sam stood and came around the counter. "Let's get it done, then."

"How much ammo we have for that gun?" John asked.

"You know, that's a good question," Clem said. "Haven't checked it out yet."

"We should check before we move it," John said. "The parking place we found is tight. Not going to be easy to move it there."

They walked down the road from the office, into a small stand of trees. The Tigr was there in the shade. When they got to it, Clem opened the tailgate and climbed inside, looking in the compartments.

"Bingo," he said, pointing at the big compartment in the floor. "Looks like about a thousand rounds. We're good for a while."

"What size?" John asked.

"It's 7.62," Clem said. "What the hell are these things?" He held up a belt of large rounds.

"Holy shit!" Sam said. "Those are 30 mm grenades for an automatic launcher. There might be one of those stashed in another compartment."

"Oh," Clem said. "The mounting bar for the machine gun has an extra set of lugs, on the other side. I'll bet it mounts there."

"Yeah," Sam said. "Surprised I didn't notice that before. See that long, thin compartment against the side? Open that. The launcher is probably in there."

"I see it," Clem said. He unlatched it. "Yep, here it is. You know how to work these?"

"Yeah, basically," Sam said. "They're similar to the American M-19s. How many grenades are there?"

"Looks like fifteen to twenty in this compartment," Clem said, "but I've only looked in about half of the compartments. This sucker was designed to be out in the field for a while."

"Maybe we shouldn't just position this thing in one place," Sam said. "Maybe we ought to use it for offense. How much fuel is in it?"

"Three-quarters of a tank," Clem said, "but I have no idea what it takes."

"What do you have in mind?" John asked.

"If we could blow up some of their trucks in that pass south of here, it'll take a while for them to clear it. Meanwhile we could alert the CHP. Have them get the Air Force out there."

"Blow them up where they sit," Clem said. "Beautiful but risky."

"Sure this is a good idea?" John asked.

"Might be our only chance," Sam said. "If we try to hunker down and use this vehicle for defense, it won't be long before we have a flood of enemy fighters swarming us. We'll get overrun in a hurry. Better to make a problem for them miles away from here."

"He's right, John," Clem said. "The bad guys probably have a bunch of these. They'll neutralize our capability in minutes. Then we're down to hunting rifles and handguns."

"Okay, I get it," John said. "You've already got a plan in mind, don't you?"

Sam nodded yes. "Sid up yet?"

"Don't know," Clem said. "It's late enough. He should be pretty well rested by now."

"Go get him and meet me in the clubhouse," Sam said.

Clem nodded and walked towards Sid's coach. John followed Sam into the clubhouse.

"What are you gonna do?" John asked.

"Check out that pass with Google Earth," Sam said as he sat in front of the PC. "I want to see if there's a good vantage point for Sid to watch, and a good place for us to hide out in the Tigr until it's time to blast the enemy."

"What's up, guys?" Sid asked, walking in with Yvonne.

"Get enough sleep?" John asked.

"Yeah," Sid said.

"Well, almost enough," Yvonne said. "What's up?"

"We got some bad news from the CHP," Sam said. "The US Army suffered a defeat south of the border, right by the entrance point for the enemy. Now they're streaming in. Be here before too long."

"Oh no," Yvonne said. "What are we gonna do? Leave?"

"You know that tight pass about twenty miles southeast of here?" Sam asked.

Sid grinned. "Yeah. If we bottle that up, there's no way around it for miles and miles. We'd need some explosives to do anything, though. A lot of explosives."

"My plan is to blow up some of their trucks in the pass," Sam said.

"With what?" Sid asked.

"The automatic grenade launcher we found in the Tigr," Clem said.

A smile washed over Sid's face. "Good idea. You guys want us to spot for you, huh?"

"Exactly," Clem said.

"You know good vantage points there?" John asked.

"As a matter of fact, yes," Sid said.

"Where?" Yvonne asked.

"Remember where we took that deer last season? It was right by the pass. There's lots of good cover overlooking the road. Hell, once things start up, we can pick off a lot of these creeps, and shoot out the tires on the vehicles you don't blow up."

"They'll get through eventually, though," Yvonne said.

"I'm hoping that the CHP will be able to bring the Air Force in to pound them," Sam said.

"Even if that doesn't happen, it will slow them down," John said. "And it's not right on top of this place."

"When do we have to go?" Yvonne asked.

"Now," Sam said. "Or they'll get through there before we're ready."

"If they haven't already," John said.

"We've got to do this," Sid said, looking at Yvonne. "You in?"

Yvonne sighed. "Yeah, I'm in. Let's go get the Jeep loaded up."

"I'll go talk to Connie," Sam said. "Ask her to call the CHP and let them know what we're doing."

"Guess I'd better go talk to Sarah," John said.

"She ain't gonna be happy," Clem said.

"If I explain to her that we'd die trying to defend this place, she'll come around," John said.

"Meet me at the front gate in ten minutes," Sam said.

{ 13 }

Pick Up

Morgan looked at Robbie, eyes wide with fear. He looked down the stairs from the kitchen. Steve was at the foot of the stairs looking up at him.

"You know a lot of the roads are locked down, right?" Robbie said. "Is Colleen in danger where she is?"

"She thinks she is," Steve said. "I don't know."

"Where is she?" Morgan asked.

"Not very far," Steve said. "Hermosa. She's on Prospect, just the other side of Aviation. Don't remember hearing that was closed, and we can get there on side roads."

"So the only big street we'll have to cross is Aviation," Robbie said. "Not so bad. We can take Harriman Lane. Pick an easy way to get across Aviation. Probably Stanford Avenue, where Big Lots is."

"Yeah," Steve said. "That'll work. She's a few doors down from the Hermosa View Elementary School."

"I can go, can't I?" Morgan asked.

"Sure," Robbie said. "It should be pretty safe. Residential streets around here should be okay."

"When can we leave?" Steve asked.

"Now," Robbie said.

"Okay, I'll drive," Steve said.

"I'll get my wallet and keys," Robbie said.

"I'll grab my purse, too," Morgan said. "Should I bring the pistol?"

"Yeah, you do that, and I'll bring one of my dad's pistols too."

Morgan and Robbie rushed into the master bedroom to get their things, then took the stairs to the front door. They got into Steve's car and backed down the driveway, eyes darting around. Robbie and Morgan were in the back.

"Nobody around," Robbie said. He put his hand on Morgan's thigh to calm her.

"We have to cross Grant," Steve said.

"That's not a major street, it's residential," Robbie said as they pulled up to the stop light. The light turned green right away and they drove across.

"One big street down," Steve said. They turned right on Harriman Lane.

"Hey, man, move down to Marshallfield Lane," Robbie said, "when you get to Harkness Lane."

"Why?" Steve asked.

"Easy way to get to Stanford," Robbie said. "The streets get weird down there."

"Oh, yeah," Steve said. "Forgot. This isn't my stomping grounds."

"I see people peeking out windows at us," Morgan said. "It's kinda creepy."

They passed block after block, most of them with stop signs.

"I hate driving in here," Morgan said. "Drive. Stop. Drive. Stop."

Robbie laughed. "Pain in the neck, but it does keep the streets a little less busy."

"I'm with Morgan," Steve said. "That's why I like Torrance better than Redondo."

"Harkness is coming up," Robbie said.

"See it." Steve made the left, then turned right when they got to Stanford.

"All these tall skinny houses," Morgan said. "Had a friend who lived in one. It was like a boxcar."

"Yeah, they build them right to the lot lines, too," Robbie said. "They're expensive now."

"Here's Aviation," Steve said as he pulled up to the stoplight. He looked down the road on both sides. "Don't see any roadblocks."

"Can't see past the curves," Robbie said. "I'll bet you can't go past Artesia to the north."

"PCH is closed too, so that bottles up the other end," Morgan said.

"Yep," Steve said. The light changed, and he moved forward. "So far so good. He made a left turn on Palm Lane, then took the 15th Street jog and turned right on Prospect. "Welcome to Hermosa."

"The signs change, huh?" Morgan asked.

"Yeah, and the price goes up," Robbie said.

"And the roads get worse," Steve said. "Wonder why that is?"

"Hermosa used a lot of concrete on its roads way back in the day," Robbie said. "And it's moved around over the years, so it's rough to drive on. Asphalt takes more maintenance, but in an earthquake zone like this it's not such a bad thing."

"That's the house," Steve said, pointing to a small, run down beach shack.

"Looks like a tear-down," Robbie said as they parked. "Want us to go to the door with you?"

"Yeah," he said. "Bring your guns."

"Why?" Morgan asked. "Is there something you didn't tell us about this?"

"Colleen said the guy she's with won't let her leave," Steve said. "We might have to force him."

"Now you tell us," Robbie said. "Think he's armed?"

"Colleen didn't think he was," Steve said, "but he's big."

Robbie snickered. "Then maybe we should let you fight him. Impress your girl."

"That's mean." Morgan chuckled.

"C'mon," Steve said, opening his door. They all got up and took the walkway through the dead scraggly lawn. A pretty young woman peeked out the window and smiled. The door opened quietly.

"Thank God," Colleen whispered, brushing her brilliant red hair back from her freckled face.

"Shut that door," a gruff voice yelled from further inside the house.

"C'mon," she whispered, stepping out. They turned to walk back to the car when a big man rushed out the door, grabbing Steve's shirt.

"What do you think you're doing?" the man shouted, his eyes crazy.

"Let go of him," Robbie said.

The man laughed. "Or else what, punk?"

Robbie pulled his .45 and pointed it at him. Morgan pulled her .38 and pointed it at him too.

"Let go," Robbie said.

The man let go and backed away, hands up. "All right, all right."

"Let's get out of here," Colleen said.

"You guys get in the car while I cover this creep," Robbie said.

Steve and Colleen rushed to the car. Morgan and Robbie stood still with their guns pointed. Steve started the car. "C'mon, guys," he yelled.

"Go," Robbie said. Morgan ran to the car, getting into the passenger side rear. Robbie backed up slowly to the car and got in as Morgan pointed her pistol out the window to cover him. Then Steve punched it. The big man rushed inside.

"You don't think he's going to follow us, do you?" Steve asked.

"He might," Colleen said. "I'd make a couple of quick turns, just in case."

"Yeah," Steve said as he drove back onto 15th Street.

"Don't go where there's a traffic light," Robbie said. "You'll get stuck."

"Who is he, anyway?" Steve asked.

"My mom's ex-boyfriend," she said. "He's been after me for a long time. Always used to walk in on me in the shower and stuff when we lived with him."

"Where's your mom?" Morgan asked. "Oh, hi, I'm Morgan."

"Nice to meet you," Colleen said. "Mom's in jail. Long story."

"Make a right on Aviation and a left on Harper," Robbie said. "Fast."

"Got it," Steve said, making a wild turn onto Aviation, which was still empty, and turning left quickly.

"Take Marshallfield back," Robbie said.

Gunfire erupted behind them.

"Crap, that's full auto," Steve said, speeding up.

"Keep going," Robbie shouted. "There's Marshallfield."

"Who's shooting?" Morgan asked.

"Either the National Guard or Islamist fighters," Robbie said. "They're the only groups I know of who have machine guns."

"Why were you with that guy?" Morgan asked.

"He convinced my boss that he was taking me to safety," Colleen said. "I pitched a fit, but everybody was too worried about their own selves by that time."

"Did he hurt you?" Steve asked.

"Not yet, but it was coming," she said. "He was trying seduction, but I wasn't having it, and he was getting pissed. He would have forced himself on me."

"Oh, geez," Morgan said.

"Thanks for getting me," Colleen said, looking at Steve. "How did you find my number? Don't remember giving it to you."

"I called Kelly," he said. "I figured she'd have it."

"Oh," Colleen said. "You were looking for me?"

"Yeah," Steve said. "Hope you don't mind."

"Not even a little bit," Colleen said, flashing her sweet smile at him.

"Good, almost to Rindge already," Robbie said.

"Where are we going?" Colleen asked.

"Robbie's place," Steve said.

"Actually my parent's place," Robbie said

"They home?" Colleen asked.

"No, they escaped in their motor home before things got so crazy."

"You were living at home?" Colleen asked.

"I had an apartment in Gardena," Robbie said. "Got overrun by the gangs. We got out just in time."

"I was living there too," Morgan said.

"You two are together?" Colleen asked.

Robbie and Morgan shot each other a glance.

"Yes," Morgan said softly.

"You two lived together before all of this?" Colleen asked.

"No, we were just neighbors," Robbie said.

Colleen giggled, looking at him. "Yeah, but you liked her, didn't you? I can tell by the way you look at her."

"Don't say it," Morgan said.

"Don't say what?" Robbie asked.

"That I'm out of your league," she said.

Colleen laughed. "Oh, brother. That again. What is it with guys?"

"No comment," Robbie said.

Steve laughed nervously.

"Aren't we going into a worse area than where I was?" Colleen asked.

"A little, maybe, but you don't have that guy to deal with anymore," Steve said, "and it's defendable."

More automatic gunfire started to the south. Everybody looked in that direction, Steve refocusing on the road after a split second.

"I don't like this," Morgan said, sliding closer to Robbie.

"Me neither," Colleen said. "How much further?"

"We're close," Robbie said. "Take Phelan Lane across Grant. No traffic lights. Our friend might be around."

"Yeah," Steve said. He took the left turn, going down a few short blocks until he hit Grant Avenue, looking west before he made the right turn. There were several Humvees coming down the street at a fast clip.

"Haul ass, dammit," Robbie said. "You have to make it to my street. Get into the driveway and out of sight before they figure out where we went."

Steve punched it, the car bouncing as it went past a dip. He made the sharp right, tires squealing, then turned into the driveway and drove back fast, tucking his car into the overhang over the garage door.

"Good, we're out of sight of the road," Robbie said. "C'mon, let's get inside."

They all got out of the car and rushed through the front door, trying to catch their breaths in front of the stairs. The front bedroom door opened and Gil peeked out, rifle in hand.

"What's going on?" he asked. "Where did you guys go?"

"We went to pick up Colleen," Steve said.

"That girl you're in love with at work?" Gil asked. Steve's face showed embarrassment. He glanced at Colleen, who looked shocked.

"Why didn't you tell me?" Colleen asked.

"Didn't seem like you were interested," Steve said.

"You could've *asked* me," she said. "I would've gone out with you."

"Really?"

"Hey, where's Justin?" Robbie asked. "His car isn't in the driveway."

"Probably good thing it wasn't, or mine would be visible from the street," Steve said.

"What happened out there?" Gil asked. "You guys look pretty shook up."

"Humvee's were blasting down Grant when we crossed," Robbie said. "We'll tell you the whole story in a little while. What's up with Justin?"

"Oh yeah, sorry," Gil said. "His boss called, asked him to go to work for a while. He took Killer with him."

"Killer?" Colleen asked.

"Justin's pit bull," Morgan said. "He's the sweetest dog."

"It's dangerous out there," Robbie said. "What if he gets pulled over?"

"His boss gave him a code for the National Guard," Gil said.

"Really," Robbie said. "I guess things will open back up after martial law is in place, then."

"Let's go upstairs," Steve said. "We have a better sight-line up there."

"Show Colleen around first," Morgan said. "Give her a chance to get her bearings."

Steve got a sheepish look on his face. "Sure, let's do that."

"Lead the way," Colleen said, taking his arm. Robbie and Morgan went up the stairs, Gil back in his room.

"Now, where were we?" Morgan asked Robbie. "Before we had to take off?"

Robbie got a smile on his face. "I think we were talking about a kiss."

"Well," she said. Robbie took her into his arms and kissed her passionately, pushing her against the wall next to the kitchen.

They broke the kiss and looked into each other's eyes.

"I had that on my mind the whole time we were gone," Robbie said.

"Me too," Morgan said, her hand touching his cheek. "Think anybody will notice if we retire to your room?"

"It's *our* room," Robbie said. "Let's wait until tonight, though, okay?"

"Why?"

"This is the early part of our relationship. Let's live with the anticipation for a while."

She moved in for another kiss, taking the lead, then looked into his eyes. "I like that idea."

***

"You're trembling," Sid said, glancing at Yvonne as he drove their Jeep towards the rocky pass.

"Of course," she said. "We might not live through this."

"We will," Sid said. "Trust me."

"Trust me?" Yvonne asked. "Is that a *Hollywood* trust me?"

"No." Sid chuckled, looking at her. "This is what I love about you. You always have a sense of humor."

"Watch the road," Yvonne said.

"I am," he said.

"You think this is gonna work?"

"Depends on what you mean," Sid said. "Do I believe that we can bottle up enemy trucks in that pass? Yeah."

"There's a *but* coming."

"It's a temporary fix. Unless the US Army shuts off the flow, the RV Park is in trouble. We might have to leave. *All of us.*"

"Some won't go," Yvonne said. "There's some older people who have nothing other than their mobile homes. They have no place to go."

"I know, that's why I didn't want to leave before," Sid said. "Some of the folks living in those park models are tribal people, you know. Not from our tribe, but still."

Yvonne glanced over with a look that smacked of shame. "Remember what I said. I don't feel it's our duty to die for these folks if they won't leave. You gonna be okay with that?"

"Let's focus on the task at hand," Sid said. "Maybe it'll be enough."

"Doubtful, but okay," she said. "Slow down, that's the place. See it coming up?"

"Yeah," Sid said. He drove the Jeep onto the dirt road and back in amongst the hillside and bushes. "This ought to do it."

They got out of the Jeep and went to the tailgate.

"You think they're close?" Yvonne asked.

"Hard to say," Sid said. "Maybe. If they'd already been through here, I think we'd know it. We would've run into them on the road."

The two scurried up the trail that led to the ridge. The heat of the day was ramping up fast.

"Hope we brought enough water," Yvonne said.

"I hope we brought enough bullets."

"Very macho thing to say." Yvonne snickered. "You would have been a hit around the campfire."

"Oh, please," he said. "Look, the good place is right up there."

"I see it. Surprised I remember it. Been a few years."

"Yes, it has," Sid said as he dropped his ammo box and took his rifle sling off his shoulder. "Perfect view. Perfect place for an ambush."

"Yeah, unless you're totally outgunned," she said. "Like we are."

"Sam's in the Tigr," Sid said.

"We stole *one,* but I'll bet the enemy has lots more," Yvonne said. "I wouldn't want to trade places with Sam and the others. At least we'll be hard to hit up here."

"True," Sid said, checking his rifles. "Glad I sighted this scope in recently."

Yvonne checked her rifles, both of which were iron-sighted. "Never did that well with scopes."

"You're a natural," Sid said. "Wish I was. I can't hit the way you can without the wonders of modern technology. Not at this age, anyway."

"We just wait now, right?" Yvonne asked.

"Yep, we wait," Sid said.

They sat together, watching the road silently.

"Sid?"

"Yeah."

"How come you didn't choose to live on the reservation? It would've been an easy life."

"I won't be *kept*," he said.

"You aren't *kept* on the reservation. Not for years and years."

"Still the way I look at it," he said.

"Then why are you such good friends with all these white men?"

Sid laughed. "You mean John and Sam and Harry and Clem? They're my brothers."

"Their ancestors forced us onto the reservation," Yvonne said.

"Yes, you're right, their ancestors did that. And my ancestors killed their ancestors' women and children, sometimes for fun."

"It never bothers you?"

"Do you control what your ancestors did?" Sid asked.

"It's the principle…"

"Answer the question," Sid said.

"No," she said. "Now you make me feel ashamed. I love Sarah and Connie and Nancy like sisters."

"What matters is what *they* do, not what their ancestors did. Besides, not every white man of the past killed Indians. Some were friends of our people."

"Did I ever tell you how wise you are?" Yvonne asked.

"Oh, please," Sid said. "I tricked you into marrying me. That's enough."

Yvonne laughed hard, then covered her mouth because of the sound. "Is that what you think?"

"Of course," he said with a child-like grin. "You're everything to me, you know."

"What's that squeaking noise?"

"You've got better ears than me," he said. "Where's it coming from?"

"Down there."

"Oh shit," Sid said. "I've got to call Sam. Hope we got cell coverage up here."

"Why?" Yvonne asked.

"Those sound like tanks to me. We ain't gonna do anything to those."

14

Boulders

T hey sat on the rocky ridge, listening to the squeaking of an approaching vehicle.

"Tanks?" Yvonne asked. "Are you sure?"

"We'll see them in a second," Sid said, watching them pass below the rocky cliff they sat on.

The squeaking got louder, and the vehicle came into view.

"That's not a tank," Sid said. "It's mobile artillery."

"What does that mean?" Yvonne asked.

"It means Sam can damage it with that grenade launcher," Sid said. "I'll call him." He pulled the phone from his pocket and hit Sam's contact.

"Sid, what's up?" Sam asked.

"There's a half-track mobile artillery vehicle heading up the convoy. Just came into view. You'll need to take it out before it can fire on you."

"Got it," Sam said. "Only one?"

"Looks like it. Oh, here come the trucks. Troop transport type again. Get ready."

"How fast are they coming?" Sam asked.

"Very slowly," Sid said. "Because of that half-track."

Sam chuckled. "It's probably their roadblock insurance. We'll be ready. How many trucks you see?"

"Hey, honey, did you count the trucks?" Sid asked.

"About a dozen," she said, still watching. "Might be more coming."

"About a dozen," Sid said into the phone.

"Okay, we'll be ready," Sam said.

Sid ended the call and put his phone back in his pocket. "He's ready."

"I hope so," Yvonne said. "What should we do? Just watch?"

"Yeah, until they come back this way. We should hear fireworks any minute. Then we need to take out the first few vehicles."

"Got it," she said.

There were two explosions, followed by automatic weapons fire.

"Here it starts," Sid said. "Be ready." Sid stretched out and put his rifle's scope to his eye. Yvonne got ready with her rifle. More explosions went off below, and more machine gun fire, punctuated by other small arms fire.

"He's got it stopped," Sid said. "Never heard the artillery piece fire."

"Here they come," Yvonne said, squeezing off a shot into the cab of the first fleeing truck. It went into the ditch and rolled sideways, men flying out. Sid fired at them, hitting several before they could find cover. Yvonne shot into the cab of the second truck, killing the driver and passenger. That truck slammed into the first one and burst into flames, blocking the road.

"Perfect," Sid said. He fired more rounds at the men running around when a third truck showed up. Yvonne opened up on that one, hitting the driver and passenger again. Then there was a shot at them, chipping a rock about twenty yards down from Yvonne's position.

"They have a pretty good idea where we are," Yvonne shouted as she reloaded.

"Hitting us is another matter," Sid said as he squeezed off shots, blowing the tires of the first three trucks. "We need to move to a better position to hit the trucks behind that first bend."

More grenade explosions went off, along with more machine gun fire.

"Sam's chasing them into the pass," Sid said as they moved farther down the ridge.

"Look, there's all the trucks," Yvonne said.

"Keep your head down," Sid said. "They're all going to be firing at us now."

"Got it," she said as she laid down and aimed. She fired off several rounds, dropping two Islamists, the rest of them snapping their heads towards the gunfire in a panic. Then a truck in the midst of them blew up as a grenade went into the back of it and exploded. Men on fire piled out screaming.

"Watch out, they're aiming up here," Sid said, getting down. A volley of fire came, chipping rocks all around them. "Get down!"

"I am down," Yvonne said, continuing to fire at the enemy. "Draw their attention up here, dammit. That way Sam and the others can do more damage with that grenade launcher."

"On it," Sid said, getting prone and firing his weapon, sighting easily with his scope. "This is like shooting fish in a barrel. They're so shook up now that they aren't even shooting at us."

Another explosion went off below, blowing up another truck, spinning it into two others.

"That's a mess," Yvonne said. "Gonna take days to clear that."

"We don't want to let any of them live if we can help it," Sid said.

Another grenade went off, and then a volley of machine gun fire from the Tigr, the remainder of the men running into view. Sid and Yvonne fired on them, hitting as many as they could before they ran the other way. Then the machine gun on the Tigr started again, along with other small arms fire.

"There's Sam!" Yvonne said. "Chasing them down with his M-16. He's fast."

"Guess he didn't forget his training after all," Sid said, eye against the scope. He fired several rounds, hitting men who were fleeing up the hillside.

"I see the Tigr now," Yvonne said. "Clem's on the machine gun. John's driving."

The gunfire went on for another minute or two, and then there was silence. Sid's phone rang. He pulled it out of his pocket and put it to his ear.

"Sam, you get 'em all?"

"Yeah," Sam said. "We're gonna gather up weapons and ammo and get the hell out of here."

"You call the CHP?"

"Nah, we don't need the Air Force to take them out," Sam said, "and if we call them they'll just open the road back up. I think we ought to make sure this stays closed for as long as possible."

"Yeah, there's no good way around this pass. Too bad we can't bring some rocks down to seal it up better. There's a few boulders in this pass that would be easy enough to break loose."

"Ask him about that artillery piece," Yvonne said. "I bet that would do it."

"Oh, yeah, how about the artillery piece? Any chance it'll still fire?"

Sam chuckled. "Great minds think alike. Clem is looking it over now. I don't think it's too badly damaged. We can probably fire off some rounds with it."

"How did you stop it?" Sid asked.

"Fired a grenade at the gunner's seat. Blew pieces of him all over the place, and machine gunned the rest of the crew."

There was squeaking below. "Hell, I can hear it," Sid said. "Clem got it going."

"Son of a bitch, he sure did," Sam said. "Got to go. You guys mind staying up there for a while, just in case somebody else shows up?"

"Sure, no problem," Sid said. He ended the call and slipped his phone back in his pocket.

"They're gonna blow some of the boulders with the artillery?" Yvonne asked.

"Yeah, Clem's working on it. That old coot can fix anything."

"I've noticed," Yvonne said. "We better get down a little further. There's gonna be rock chips flying everywhere when he opens up with that sucker."

"Yeah, I hope those guys take cover down there. Once a big rock starts rolling, who knows where it'll go."

Suddenly there was a loud boom, and rock chips flew out around the bottom of a house-sized boulder on the far side of the canyon.

"Holy crap!" Sid said, getting his head down. There was another boom, and the boulder started to roll, crashing down the hillside, gaining speed, slamming into the broken trucks on the road below.

"Wow!" Yvonne said. "Who's going to clean that up?"

Sid chuckled. "I'd better peek at the south side of the road. Maybe we ought to move over there."

"Good idea," Yvonne said. "I know just the place."

"Where we got the big horn a few years ago?"

"That's it," Yvonne said. They moved further down the ridge, until they had a good view of the road heading south, past the bend.

"Perfect," Sid said. "I can see more than a mile." Another boom came from the canyon.

"They're working on that other big boulder," Yvonne said. "That'll make this into a month-long cleanup job."

"Hell, it'll take longer than that," Sid said, laughing. "My dad worked on roads back in the day. You know how they had to clear big rocks like that?"

"No, how?"

"Jack hammered them into moveable pieces. Took a long time. It's harder than breaking up cement."

Another big boom went off, and then the crashing sound as a huge boulder came down, dust filling the air even where they were.

"That had to be bigger than the first one," Yvonne said. "Watch your eyes. Might want to close them for a few minutes."

"Already did," Sid said. There was another boom.

"Damn, they're really going to town," Yvonne said.

"I'd better open my eyes," Sid said. "Gotta look down the road. There's gonna be more enemy coming."

"How far do they have to go to get around this?" Yvonne asked.

Sid laughed. "This is a big problem for them. They'd have to pick up I-8 around Yuma if they want to come into San Diego from the back way. I'll bet that's guarded well. The only other alternative they have is to stay in Mexico until they're west of the Otay preserve, and then they get into the area where we actually have a wall on the border."

"So we've screwed them over well," Yvonne said. "Good."

"Yeah, pretty much," Sid said, opening his eyes just as another boom went off. Then there was the crashing noise, louder this time. The ground beneath them shook as the boulder hit the bottom.

"Holy crap, close your eyes again," Yvonne shouted. "That was HUGE."

Rock chips flew into the air, raining down around them.

"Wow!" Sid said. "That ought to hold it."

"Seriously," Yvonne said. When the sound of rocks hitting the ground stopped, she slowly opened her eyes. "Look, here comes another convoy."

"They're slowing down fast. They must see the mess."

"We're going to take them out, right?"

"Hell yeah," Sid said, moving the rifle into position. "Come to papa."

"That's quite a few trucks," Yvonne said. "Dammit, got dirt in my eyes again.

"I'm good," Sid said, pulling the trigger, splattering the head of the driver in the lead, causing his truck to swerve and spin sideways. The trucks following slammed on the brakes, but it was too late. Three trucks slammed into the lead truck as Sid fired into the cabs of all of them. Yvonne opened up, hitting the truck cabs as far back as she could. Men from the backs of the first few trucks ran away in a panic as the other trucks tried to turn around.

"Shoot their tires," Sid said.

"What about the men?" Yvonne asked.

"Actually, you take them. I'll take the tires."

"Okay." Yvonne fired several times, hitting men with all but the last shot.

Sid nailed the tires on several of the trucks, but two of them got turned around, men running to catch them and jump in the back. He hit a few of them as the trucks rolled away, but he couldn't hit the tires.

"Some of them are gonna get away," Yvonne said.

"I know, but there isn't a way they can get around this mess," Sid said. "They'll go back home. Probably re-route their people if they can."

"We're gonna need somebody here to keep an eye out, aren't we?"

"I don't think so, sweetie," Sid said. "They won't be able to go this way. I don't know what that last boulder looks like, but I suspect we just created a several-month problem."

Sid's phone rang. He pulled it out and answered it.

"Hey, Sam, what the hell did you guys blow back there? It shook the ground when it hit."

Sam snickered. "We didn't mean to make that big of a mess. That last boulder was a lot bigger than it looked, and it brought down a lot of dirt and several other boulders when it broke loose. They won't be getting through this way for months. Heard you guys firing. Another convoy?"

"Yeah," Sid said. "About ten trucks. We wasted all but the last two. They high-tailed it."

"Good," Sam said. "I wouldn't worry about the ones that got away. They won't be able to come through here again."

"Should we hang around up here for a while?"

"I don't see why. Meet you at the mouth of the canyon."

"Great, thanks," Sid said. He put his phone back in his pocket.

"We leaving?" Yvonne asked.

"Yep," Sid said. "C'mon."

They started down from the ridge.

***

Ji-Ho came into the living room. "Good afternoon," he said. "How doing?"

"Great," Kaylee said. "How are you, uncle?"

"Slept like baby," he said. "Trevor up yet?"

"Nope," Seth said. "Maybe I should go wake him up."

"Not a bad idea," Angel said. "Getting late."

Seth got up and walked towards the bedroom hall.

"Hey Emma, let's go see what we can cook for dinner, okay?" Kaylee said.

"Sure." Emma stood up and followed her into the kitchen.

Seth came back in the living room. "Trevor's getting dressed. He was already awake."

"Good," Ji-Ho said.

"Is Emma a good cook, man?" Matt asked, looking at Seth.

"She's good at what she knows how to make," Seth said. "Makes great scalloped potatoes."

"Yum," Jamie said. "Too bad we didn't bring swim suits. That pool looks really good."

Ji-Ho laughed. "Yeah, nice out there. We should go check out my rooftop deck. You can see long way out on ocean. Good place to have drink."

"I'm game," Matt said.

"Me too," Seth said.

"Me three," Angel said.

Jamie snickered. "Which of you guys is Curley?"

"What mean *Curley?*" Ji-Ho asked.

"He's talking about the Stooges," Matt said. "Remember when we watched them that time?"

"Oh, old black and white comedy," Ji-Ho said, grinning. "I like."

They walked towards the stairs, climbing them into a loft area with a three-sixty-degree view. There was a spiral staircase against the far wall.

"Maybe that's why he and Trevor get along so well," Seth said. "They're both Three Stooges fans.

"Trevor brilliant," Ji-Ho said. "He in college?"

"Nah, he wants to be a gunsmith," Seth said. "Parent's couldn't afford to pay for a four-year college. He went to Crenshaw Tech, got an AA degree."

"Crenshaw Tech?" Ji-Ho asked.

Matt snickered. "He's talking about El Camino Community College."

"But they live in South Bay, right? Must have some money. Expensive around here."

"They do," Seth said, "but white middle-class kids don't get help very easily here in Taxafornia, and it costs so much to own a house here that there's usually not money left for the kid's college. The high taxes pay for non-producer families to send their kids free. It's not fair."

Angel laughed. "Here it comes. Gringo."

Seth cracked up. "Yeah, whatever. It *is* harder for middle-class kids unless their grades all the way through High School are perfect. His weren't. Too much weed."

"Should be by merit only," Ji-Ho said. "California bad now unless very well-off. Maybe when this over I'll talk to him. I have no kids. I'd put him through school. Plenty money. Kaylee too."

"You're a really nice man, Ji-Ho," Matt said.

"Let's go up spiral staircase," he said. "Watch step. I open trap door at top."

"This is going to be cool," Seth said.

"Hey, guys," Trevor said as he walked in. "Going to the roof-top deck, eh?"

"Yeah," Angel said.

"Sleep well?" Jamie asked.

"Like a baby," he said. "I don't want to get stuck here for too long, but this is a nice break from the craziness down there."

They all got up on the deck and stood at the four-foot wall that surrounded it on all sides.

"Where's the sailboats?" Trevor asked, looking around. "Perfect day for sailing."

"They stop when trouble get bad," Ji-Ho said. "I think a lot leave. Heard Catalina full up."

"Hey, what's that?" Angel asked, pointing. There was a medium sized ship way off in the distance, launching several small boats.

"Don't like that," Ji-Ho said. He went to a cabinet against the wall and opened it, pulling out a telescope. "Let's take look."

He stood by the wall and put the telescope to his eye, his brow furrowing.

"Who is it?" Matt asked. "Bad guys?"

"Islamist," Ji-Ho said. "Trevor, let's go get my long rifles."

"We can't hit them that far out, can we?" Seth asked.

"We can hit those boats," Trevor said. "They're inflatables. We'll pop them while they're on the way here. They'll sink."

Trevor and Ji-Ho raced down the spiral staircase, Jamie following. Seth picked up the telescope and looked. "Holy crap, there's a lot of guns sitting in those boats."

"Let's see," Angel said. Seth handed him the telescope and he looked. "Dammit. There's six guys in each of those boats. Heavily armed."

Trevor and Jamie rushed onto the roof, then bent down and took rifles Ji-Ho handed up, bringing them to the wall and leaning them. Ji-Ho came up with a large box of ammo and set it down, then went back down the stairs. "Trevor, need hand with the last one."

Trevor raced over and reached down, coming up with a large weapon, complete with muzzle break and tripod.

"My God, is that what I think it is?" Seth asked.

"It's a frigging Barrett M82," Trevor said as Ji-Ho set it up.

"In English," Angel said.

"It's a .50 Cal sniper rifle," Trevor said. "Those guys aren't going to survive this."

"Who want to join?" Ji-Ho asked. "Brought up 30-06 and .270 with scopes. Also varmint rifles. Shoot boats, then people."

"You first," Trevor said.

Ji-Ho grinned. "Let's see how this work." He aimed the M82 at the lead boat and opened fire while Seth watched through the telescope.

"Holy crap, that first boat is sinking already."

Trevor opened up with the .270, hitting two of the men in the boat. The others swam frantically towards the other boats as Ji-Ho fired at them.

"Nice shooting," Seth said, watching two more of the five boats sink.

"Three to go. Start shooting men in water."

Seth put down the telescope and picked up one of the rifles, getting next to Trevor on the wall. Jamie and Angel picked up rifles too, and they all blazed away at the men in the water as Ji-Ho shot the last three boats, sinking them quickly.

There was a flash from the enemy ship.

"Crap, they going to shoot at us?" Seth asked.

"That reflection from telescope," Ji-Ho said. "They looking for us. Might be able to hit big boat. I try."

"Don't bother, the US Navy is coming," Jamie said, looking through the telescope.

Suddenly there was a boom, and an explosion on the enemy ship. It listed slightly.

"Navy have them," Ji-Ho said, grinning. "Guess I let them handle."

The navy boat fired its gun again, hitting the ship broadside, causing a large explosion. The boat sank quickly.

"Wow," Ji-Ho said. "Let's see telescope."

Jamie handed it to him.

"Not many survivors in water," Ji-Ho said.

"Yeah," Trevor said.

"Wonder if anybody's going to tell the navy where we are?" Matt asked.

"They might," Angel said. "Might not be a good thing."

Kaylee stuck her head cautiously out the trap door. "What happened? Emma is scared to death. So am I."

"Enemy trying to land five rubber boats," Ji-Ho said. "We stop."

"That was really loud," Kaylee said. "We might have a visit from the police."

"No matter," Ji-Ho said. "Police chief my friend. I call him. Be down in minute."

"Seth, you should come down and be with Emma," Kaylee said. "She's really upset."

"Okay," Seth said. "You okay?"

"No," she said. "Matt, get over here."

"I'm coming," Matt said.

15

Warning

Steve and Colleen climbed the stairs.

"Still showing her around, huh?" Morgan said, a sly smile on her face. "Where are you sleeping tonight?"

Robbie looked at Morgan and shook his head, a snicker escaping.

"Be nice, you guys," Steve said. Colleen looked at him, eyes dancing.

"You always embarrass so easily," she said, brushing his hair away from his eyes.

"I know, sorry," he said. "Let's check out the kitchen and dining room."

"Okay," Colleen said, taking his hand. Steve looked at it, then at her face. "What?"

"You're beautiful," he whispered.

"That's more like it," she said, getting closer to him as they walked through the archway into the kitchen.

"You see that?" Morgan whispered. "She's got him, and he doesn't even know yet."

Robbie snickered. "Yeah, looks that way. He's talked about this girl quite a bit over the last few months. I can see why. She's cute."

"Hey," Morgan said.

"What? I'm not saying I'm interested in her," Robbie said.

Morgan giggled. "Somebody else doesn't even know yet," she said, taking him back into her arms. They kissed passionately in the hall, Steve and Colleen walking in on them.

"That looks like fun," Colleen whispered. "Where *are* we sleeping tonight, anyway. That back bedroom?"

"We can," Steve said.

"Good, then let's go down there," she said. "I want to be alone for a while."

They went down the stairs together, Robbie noticing them as he and Morgan finished their kiss. "There they go," he whispered.

"You think they're going to hit it off, I take it," Morgan said. "They seem to be moving pretty fast."

"They knew each other for a while," Robbie said. "Unlike you and me. What's it been now – day and a half?"

"You knew me from before," she said to him.

"I longed for you from afar," Robbie said. "We didn't talk much. Steve's spent hours with Colleen."

"Okay, I get it," Morgan said.

The front door opened. Robbie froze, then rushed to the top of the stairs. He saw Killer walk in, followed by Justin.

"Hey, man, what's up?" Robbie asked.

"My job's starting up again," he said.

"Introduce Killer to Colleen," Morgan said. "She's in the back bedroom with Steve."

"Colleen? The one he worships at work?" Justin asked, a smile on his face.

"That's the one," Robbie said. "I'd knock on the door before you go in."

"I'm jealous," Morgan said, putting her arms back around Robbie's waist. "Can't we take a nap or something?"

"Or something?" Robbie asked.

"Yeah," Morgan said. "Do I have to spell it out for you?"

"In a few minutes," Robbie said. "I want to find out what's going on outside. I'm sure Justin will fill us in as soon as he gets up here."

Morgan sighed. "Okay, I can wait, as long as it's not too long."

Killer trotted up the stairs, going directly to Morgan, nuzzling her with his massive head.

"Hi, boy," she said, petting him. Robbie came over and stroked his back as Justin trudged up the stairs.

"Glad I went to their room when I did," Justin said. "I think they're about to get busy."

"Don't tease them," Morgan said.

"Tease? I'm envious," Justin said as he plopped down onto the couch.

"So, what's happening out there?" Robbie asked.

"Crazy stuff," Justin said. "The National Guard has chased most of the Islamists out of the area, and the gangs just went home."

"So things should be getting better?" Morgan asked.

"Depends on what you mean by better," Justin said. "The state government is working closely with the Feds. They want to lock this mess down in a hurry and then get business and agriculture moving again. The country needs it to survive, with so many other places messed up. They're going to apply very tight controls."

"What kind of controls?" Robbie asked.

"First, they're going to cut the LA area into grids with checkpoints. That will keep the gangs from being able to move around and victimize people."

"Did they lay out the grids already?" Robbie asked.

"We're on the edge of one. There's a dividing line on Inglewood Ave to the east and El Segundo Blvd to the north."

"Interesting," Robbie said. "When are they gonna put this into place?"

"It'll take them a few days," Justin said. "I don't have a problem with the grids and checkpoints, actually. That's not so bad. It's the other stuff."

"What other stuff?" Morgan asked.

"Rumors, but from good sources," Justin said. "They plan to force everybody back to work, and they aren't going to allow anybody to quit or move from one job to another for a while. They want stability."

"They can't do that," Robbie said. "We aren't slaves."

"My boss thinks it's BS, but everybody else I talked to believes it."

Robbie's phone rang. He picked it up and checked the number. "Work."

"No way," Morgan said. Robbie put the phone to his ear, getting up and walking into the kitchen.

"Did you have a job before this started, Morgan?" Justin asked.

"Cocktail waitress at one of the card clubs in Gardena," she said. "Not exactly a strategic job."

"Oh, I don't know," Justin said. "Relaxing after work is important. I'll bet your job will be back in no time."

Robbie came back in and sat on the couch next to Morgan. "We're opening again, in three days. They wanted to make sure I was available."

"Even the expensive places are opening, eh?" Justin asked. "Things may be getting back to normal after all."

"Maybe," Robbie said.

"I'll probably get called too, then," Morgan said. "I'd rather not have to deal with going into Gardena."

"That's outside of the checkpoint," Justin said. "Like my job. You'll get a special card to pass by the checkpoints."

"I'm lucky, I guess," Robbie said. "My job should be in the grid."

"Where is it?" Morgan asked.

"On Sepulveda in Manhattan Beach," he said. "Just past Rosecrans."

"Very upper crust," Justin said.

"It's expensive there, that's for sure," Morgan said.

"That's not my only job," Robbie said.

"What's the other one?" Morgan asked.

"He's a writer," Justin said. "Pretty good one, too."

"Oh, really?" Morgan asked. "Why didn't you mention that before?"

"Never got around to it," Robbie said.

"What do you write?"

"Articles for two political websites, and fiction. Short stories and novels."

"You're kidding," she said. "What genre?"

"Action-adventure, Horror, and Sci-Fi," Robbie said. "I've got to work on that again tomorrow. Missed a couple days."

"You guys always make it sound like you're driven to write," Justin said. "It's so melodramatic."

"I suppose," Robbie said. "It does bother me when I can't write. Don't know why."

"I think it's cool," Morgan said. "Can I read some of your stuff?"

"Sure, but it'll make me nervous," Robbie said.

"Why?" she asked.

"Because he thinks his work sucks," Justin said. "He's wrong, of course. It's very good. Artists crack me up."

"Listen," Morgan whispered.

"Holy crap, is that Steve and Colleen?" Justin asked.

"That didn't take long," Morgan said, her expression a mixture of amusement and jealousy.

"I've got to take off for a while," Justin said. "Have to pick up some material from a vendor and take it to the shop. Mind if I leave Killer here?"

"No problem," Robbie said. "That why you came back?"

"Yeah, can't take the dog where I'm going. See you guys later." He got up and left.

"I can't take this," Morgan said, standing up. She held out her hand to Robbie.

"Can't take what?" he asked.

"That," she said, nodding towards the downstairs as Steve and Colleen got louder.

Robbie looked at her tenuously as he got to his feet.

"Oh, please," Morgan said, dragging him towards the bedroom. "It's time. I'm gonna wear you out." They went into the master bedroom and closed the door.

***

Sid and Yvonne were the first to drive through the gate into the RV Park. Connie ran out of the office to meet them.

"Where's Sam?" she asked.

"He'll be along pretty soon," Yvonne said. "Don't worry, nobody got hurt."

"We heard a few loud explosions. One of them rattled the windows."

Sid laughed. "Must have been the last boulder they brought down."

"Everything went okay here, I take it," Yvonne said.

"Yeah, it was quiet," Connie said. "Almost too quiet. What's holding up Sam?"

"He's following Clem home," Sid said.

"Clem rode with them in the Tigr," Connie said.

"We picked up a piece of mobile artillery," Yvonne said. "It's a half-track, so it's slow. Clem's driving it. Sam and John are guarding the rear."

"Oh," Connie said. "You guys got the pass closed up, obviously."

"And then some," Sid said. "We used the artillery piece to bring a bunch of boulders down on top of the ruined troop transport trucks.

It'll take months to clear it, and there's no other way through. We should be safe here for a while."

"Good," Connie said.

"Listen, here they come," Yvonne said. "Hear the squeaking?"

"I never hear things as well as you do," Sid said.

"Oh, I hear it," Connie said. "Sounds scary."

"I thought it was a tank when I heard it," Sid said. "Good thing it wasn't."

"Seriously," Yvonne said.

Sam drove through the gate in the Tigr, positioning the vehicle with its guns pointing down the road.

"Sam!" Connie cried, running to meet him. They embraced as John got out of the passenger side. The mobile artillery piece creaked into view and approached slowly.

"Where do you want this thing?" Clem asked as he rolled up.

"Good question," Sam said. "Why don't you pull it behind the clubhouse for now, so it's out of sight."

"Okay," Clem said. He drove the smelly diesel vehicle through the gate as others at the park approached to watch.

"Wow," Sarah said as she ran up. "Look at that thing."

John rushed over, taking her into his arms. "Hi, sweetie," he said.

"I'm so glad you're safe," she said, hugging him. "Nobody got hurt?"

"Not a scratch," John said. "How's Harry?"

"He's getting better pretty fast," Sarah said. "Dr. Grace just checked him out a little while ago. Nancy's still staying by his side all the time."

Clem parked the mobile artillery piece and shut down the engine. People gathered around it.

"That what was causing all the big booms?" asked one man.

"Yeah," Clem said. "This sucker puts out some noise. We brought a bunch of boulders down in the pass. The enemy won't be able to go through there for quite a while."

"That means we're safe for now?" another man asked.

"Yep, that's what it means," Clem said. "I hope anyway."

"Good spot," Sam said as he and Connie walked behind the clubhouse. "How much fuel is left in that thing?"

"Half a tank or so," Clem said. "It doesn't burn that much, but then it doesn't have much *get up and go* either."

"No, but it's got it where it counts," Sam said. "Couldn't believe what we were able to do in that pass."

"You think the authorities are gonna mess with us about that?" Sid asked. "We made a big expensive problem for them. Might as well have blown a bridge."

Sam shrugged. "I'm sure some people will be happier than others. There are a few towns on the other side of that pass."

"And now those people are trapped," said somebody in the crowd. "Great."

"It was the right thing to do, as far as I'm concerned," Clem said. "It was that or flee the area."

Sam's phone rang. He pulled it out of his pocket and looked at the number. "Officer Ryan." He answered the call. "Yeah, Ryan?"

"Can you open the gate for us? We need to talk."

"Oh, you're here?" Sam asked. "Sure, I'll be right down. Sit tight."

"They're here?" Connie asked. "They always call first."

"Yeah," Sam said, heading for his Jeep. "He sounded upset to me. Be back in a few minutes. Could you make sure we have some coffee?"

"Sure, honey," Connie said. She rushed into the office as Sam drove down the road.

"Wonder if they know about our handiwork already?" John asked.

"Maybe," Clem said.

"*Probably,*" Sid said. "They have satellite capability. They might have seen it that way, or maybe somebody trying to get north called them up."

"We best keep our mouths shut as much as possible," John said. "We might be in some trouble for what we did."

"Yeah," Clem said. They sat nervously next to the clubhouse, waiting for Sam to get back.

"John, can we go relax for a while?" Sarah asked.

"Sure, honey," he said, getting up. He followed her back to their rig.

"Maybe I should go join Yvonne," Sid said. "I could use a nap. My hours are all screwed up now."

"Yeah, you do that," Clem said. He watched Sid walk away, and then went into the clubhouse to watch TV.

Sam drove back through the gate, the CHP cruiser behind him. Officer Ryan was driving, Officer Patrick in the passenger seat. Both vehicles parked in front of the office. They rushed inside, Sam shutting the door behind them.

"Want some coffee?" Connie asked. "Got some brewing right now. Be just a minute or two."

"That would be great," Officer Patrick said.

"I think I'll pass," Officer Ryan said. "Little too late in the day for me."

"Okay, take a seat," Sam said. "What's on your mind?"

"We know about your operation," Ryan said.

"The pass?" Sam asked.

"Yeah," Ryan said. "The National Guard and the US Army are pissed."

"Why?" Connie asked.

"They wanted to trap the enemy in Jamul," Ryan said. "At least that's what they said."

"You think there's something else going on?" Sam asked.

"Yeah," Ryan said. "I think there are traitors in their midst. I think they're using the Islamists to terrorize the citizens into sitting still for their martial law plans."

"They wanted us to come arrest you guys," Patrick said, leaning back in his chair. "We refused."

"How can you refuse?" Connie asked.

"They have no jurisdiction over us," Ryan said. "The brass is behind us on this, so far."

"So why'd you come out here?" Sam asked.

"To warn you and pick your brain," Ryan said.

"Warn us about what?" Connie asked.

"You might get a visit from the National Guard," Ryan said. "They might try to confiscate your weapons."

"Dammit," Sam said.

"Don't give them your weapons," Ryan said.

"Wouldn't that cause them to shoot us?" Connie asked.

"I doubt it," Patrick said. "They're trying to get people on board for martial law. I think a massacre of citizens would make that a little bit difficult, even inside the California Government."

"So you're saying we should resist?"

"Yeah, don't let them in the gate," Ryan said. "Ask for a warrant. Tell them you'll go public if they force their way in. There is no martial law in this area. They have no authority over you guys, but if you let them in, they might grab you and your weapons."

"This is scary," Connie said. "Coffee's done." She went to the counter and poured a cup for Patrick. "You want one, honey?"

"Sure," Sam said.

"What possessed you guys to blow up that pass, anyway?" Ryan asked.

"We captured that GAZ Tigr and found that it had both the machine gun and the grenade launcher stowed in the back. I know how to operate this kind of stuff, and so does Clem."

"Clem?" Patrick asked. "That old coot?"

"Yeah," Sam said. "He helped me get the video surveillance and the gate alarm rigged up, too. Valuable guy. Even good in a fight. Anyway, we knew that Tigr and our hunting weapons wouldn't be enough to defend this place from an attack. When we heard they were going to use route 94 as a pipeline, we decided to blow up their trucks in the pass. We didn't expect to bring all the boulders and rubble down. Got that idea when we captured their mobile artillery piece."

"Mobile artillery?" Ryan asked.

"Wanna see it?" Sam asked.

"Wait, take your coffees," Connie said, bringing cups for Patrick and Sam. She poured one for herself, and they went outside, heading for the back side of the clubhouse.

"Lord have mercy," Ryan said when he saw the artillery piece. "How much damage did you do in that pass? I only saw one picture. Looked like mostly busted up trucks."

"We brought down a bunch of large boulders," Sam said. "It'll take months to clear it."

"Good," Patrick said. "That means the back door is officially closed. Screw the Feds. Screw the National Guard. This will protect the people in San Diego."

"Settle down, junior," Ryan said, glancing at Patrick.

"Sorry, boss, but this pisses me off," Patrick said. "Our job is to protect citizens, not steer public opinion by letting them get killed."

"We figure that the only remaining back way into San Diego is I-8," Sam said. "There's no reason for the enemy to backtrack to this RV Park. It's not strategic, and it's too far out of the way now."

"There *is* a reason you're forgetting about," Ryan said.

"What's that?" Connie asked.

"Revenge," Ryan said. "It *would* take them a lot of effort, though, so you might be safe for a while at least. They'll have a big problem if they try to use I-8 to enter San Diego."

"Yeah, we've got a major force guarding I-8 in Alpine," Patrick said. "No way they get through that."

"Assuming we can trust the forces there," Sam said.

"Yeah, assuming that, and I'm not comfortable at this point," Ryan said.

"What do you think is going to happen?" Connie asked.

"I think all the major population centers are going under martial law within the next week or so," Ryan said. "It's going to stop the immediate problem in most of those areas. There are still a lot of enemy fighters hiding out in north San Diego County and the Inland Empire. The battle is going to move to those areas, but at least the population there is lower. The body count won't be nearly as bad."

"You're thinking martial law is dangerous, though, aren't you?" Connie asked.

"Once you let the government use the military to take control of the population, they have a hard time giving up that power," Ryan said. "It makes things so much easier for them."

16

Enemies Foreign and Domestic

There was squeaking and bumping below them, in the rear downstairs bedroom.

"They're still going," Morgan said, turning on her back, breath still coming fast. "Listen to that."

"What?" Robbie asked, in a daze, looking at the ceiling as sweat rolled off his forehead.

"Colleen and Steve." She giggled. "I really threw you for a loop, didn't I?"

He turned his head towards her, tears forming in his eyes, which locked with hers.

"Wow," she whispered. "I haven't gotten a look like that before."

"From me?"

"From anybody," Morgan said. She used a tissue from the nightstand to dry his eyes and his forehead.

"You're right, they *are* still going," Robbie said, smiling at her.

"Think they heard us?"

"Doubt it," Robbie said. "I used to sleep down there, remember? My parents could be pretty frisky, but I never heard it. Not even once."

"Then how do you know they were frisky?"

"The way they looked at each other sometimes. Playful stuff they'd do."

"Uh oh, your dad didn't smack her butt, did he?" Morgan asked, eyes dancing.

"It kinda runs in the family," Robbie said.

"Oh, really, now?" Morgan asked. "We'll see about that." She turned towards him, laying herself partially on top of him. They kissed tenderly.

"Guess what's back," he whispered.

She looked at him silently, then straddled him, raising up, coming down while she bit her lower lip. It was slower and more tender. They drifted off to sleep afterwards.

Robbie woke later to a knocking on the door. "Yeah?" he shouted.

"You better come see this," Gil said.

"What's going on?" Morgan asked. She stretched, then got up on her elbows. "You look proud of yourself."

"I'm happy," he said as he got off the bed. "It's never been like that for me."

"You've had other girlfriends, though, haven't you?" she asked.

He watched her get out of bed and dress. She noticed him looking and smiled.

"Cat got your tongue?" she asked.

"Yes, I've had other girlfriends. Even a couple who I was in love with. This was different."

"How?" she asked.

"It's hard to describe."

"Try," she said.

"It's like I want to become part of you."

She stared into his eyes, searching, then tears came down her cheeks.

"What's wrong?" he asked.

"We feel the same way, and I know where it leads," she said.

"I don't care where it leads, I just don't want it to go away."

"Hey, you guys," Gil said from outside the door.

"Coming," Robbie said. He walked to the door, Morgan right behind him. She pulled him back right before he opened it, hugging him close and kissing him again.

"My God," Robbie said, his whole body trembling.

"I know," she whispered, looking at his face for a moment. "Let's go see what's up."

They walked out into the living room, but froze when they saw the video on the TV screen.

"Is that New York?" Morgan asked.

"Somebody floated a nuclear device into New York harbor and set it off," Gil said, looking at them with glassy eyes. "The lower part of Manhattan and a big chunk of New Jersey are gone."

"Oh no," Robbie said. "They say who did it?"

"Not yet," Gil said.

Steve and Colleen came up the stairs.

"Oh, my God, what happened?" Colleen asked.

"Somebody nuked New York City," Morgan said.

"No," Steve said. They gathered around and watched the video. Then the announcer's voice came back.

"This just in," the announcer said. *"Another device has gone off in Puget Sound, near Seattle, Washington. It appears to be a larger device than the one detonated in New York harbor."*

"No!" Colleen said. "What if they do that in LA Harbor? Will it kill all of us?"

"Probably not," Gil said. "Depends on which way the wind blows."

"The wind almost always comes from the ocean," Robbie said. "So we'd probably survive here. LA Harbor is pretty far south."

"Not that we'd want that to happen," Steve said.

"There's the understatement of the year," Gil said.

"Seattle police are working out a way to evacuate as many people as possible," the announcer said. *"Prevailing winds will probably blow the fallout east, which is going to make evacuations more difficult."*

"Who did this?" Morgan asked.

"If it wasn't the Islamists, it was somebody working with the Islamists," Gil said.

The front door opened. Killer lifted his head, and then trotted down the stairs.

"Hey, Killer," Justin said. They came up the stairs together. Justin stopped when he saw the TV screen. "Holy shit, what happened?"

"Somebody lit off nukes in New York and Seattle," Gil said.

"No way," Justin said.

"This changes everything," Robbie said. "I'll have to spend some time writing for the websites today."

"The blast in New York harbor has caused tremendous damage in lower Manhattan, Brooklyn, and Jersey City. There are no estimates of casualties there, but the numbers will be horrendous, as will the economic impact."

"Yeah, no shit," Justin said, "they saying who did it yet?"

"No," Gil said. "It just happened."

"This reminds me of 9-11," Morgan said.

"Seriously," Robbie said.

"The White House has just released a statement," the announcer said. *"We know who made these attacks possible, and they will pay a heavy price."*

"Can we go back to bed and forget about this?" Colleen asked.

Morgan flashed her a grin.

"You heard us, didn't you?" Colleen whispered. "I'm so embarrassed."

"You didn't hear us?" Morgan asked.

"No," she said. "I guess I can be a little loud. I've been storing it up for a while, though."

"Storing it up?" Steve asked.

"For you, dummy," Colleen said. "What took you so long? You could've had me a few months ago."

Morgan laughed. Steve shot her a sheepish grin.

"This just in," the announcer said. "The Port of Vladivostok in Russia has just been hit. The device was larger than the New York bomb. It appears to have been the size of the device detonated earlier today in Puget Sound."

"Well, either that was us, or Russia had nothing to do with this," Steve said.

"I didn't think it was Russia," Gil said. "They've been on our side against the rise of the Islamist Caliphate in the Middle East."

"Yeah, that's true," Robbie said. "They have a problem with terrorism there too. Worse than ours, in some ways."

"Ladies and gentlemen, we have yet another report of an attack, this time in Charleston Harbor," the announcer said. He sounded really shaken now.

"What's happening?" Colleen asked, on the verge of crying. Steve pulled her close.

"The world is going crazy," Gil said. "We're living in historic times. This is like 1939."

"More like 1941," Robbie said. "I need to write about this now. I'm gonna go set up on the kitchen table."

"Can I watch?" Morgan asked. "I won't say anything."

"Sure, but it won't be too exciting," Robbie said.

"I don't care. I want to stay close to you."

They got up.

"Can we go back to the bedroom?" Colleen asked.

"Yeah," Steve said. They got up and went down the stairs.

"This enough space for you?" Morgan asked as she followed Robbie, looking at the cluttered table.

"Sure, I'll just move things over. I used to write on this table when I was living here," he said. "When nobody was home and it was hot outside. This room has better airflow than my old bedroom does."

He set up his laptop on the table and pulled chairs over, then got to work. Morgan watched him, reading the text on the screen as his fingers flew over the keyboard. He wrote several pages, and then paused and opened up a browser, going to a message board.

"Buzz is that North Korea supplied the devices, and the Islamists placed them," Robbie said. "Not surprising to me."

"Isn't North Korea closely aligned with China?" Morgan asked. "I hear Asian people in the card clubs talking about that all the time."

Robbie chuckled. "Yeah. What is it with Asians and poker?" he asked. "I've been to the card clubs a few times. It's almost always half Asian."

"Part of their culture, I guess," Morgan said. "They tip pretty well. Do you play?"

"Poker?" Robbie asked.

"Yeah."

"I used to play online a lot until the Feds shut the good sites down," Robbie said. "I was better online than in person, but I could play well enough to win a little money at the clubs."

Gil rushed into the kitchen. "Hey, man, Russia just warned China to move its troops away from the North Korean border, or risk losing them."

"It's on," Justin said, following Gil into the kitchen.

"Yeah, that's what I'm seeing on the message boards," Robbie said. "Now get out of here so I can write this article."

"Oh, crap, he's in *writing mode* again," Gil said. He looked at Justin and snickered. They went back into the living room.

"What do they mean by *writing mode?*" Morgan asked.

"I can get a little obsessive sometimes," he said. "Don't worry, that's usually only with the fiction. I'll have this article done in a few minutes. Want to proof read it for me?"

"Sure," she said, her eyes lighting up.

Robbie concentrated on the article, eyes on the screen as his fingers rushed over the keyboard. Morgan watched silently for almost ten minutes.

"There," Robbie said. He turned towards her and saw her expression. "What?"

"This is you," she said. "Isn't it?"

"Yes," he said. "Not too late to back out."

"Are you kidding me?" she asked. "Move over so I can proof it for you."

Robbie rolled his chair away and Morgan rolled hers in front of the laptop screen. She read silently, putting a pound sign by problems she saw. After a few minutes she turned to him and smiled. "Done. Caught a few things."

"Thanks," he said. She showed him where the typos and misspelled words were, and he fixed them on the fly.

"You're a good editor," Robbie said. "Thanks."

"You're brilliant, you know," Morgan said, looking him in the eye.

"No I'm not," Robbie said. "I'm kind of a hack, but at least I'm good enough to get paid a little, and I love doing it."

Morgan shook her head. "I'm anxious to read your fiction."

Robbie's face turned red. He got back in front of the laptop screen and published the piece, then pushed himself away from the table.

"Listen. There they go again," Morgan whispered.

"Yeah," he said. "Steve's in love with her. I knew that before we met her."

"Because of the way he talked about her?"

"Yeah," Robbie said. "We've been pushing him to get up the courage to talk to her. He's painfully shy."

"Yeah, I can tell," Morgan said, "but look who's talking. You could have had me months ago too, you know."

"We're heading into a crazy time," Robbie said. "You know that, right?"

"I know that," she said. "Better to be together than apart."

Morgan's cellphone rang. "Be right back." She raced out into the living room and grabbed it off the coffee table.

"*Hemingway* done in there?" Gil asked. Justin snickered.

"Yeah," she said, putting the phone to her ear as she went back into the kitchen. Robbie watched her have a quick conversation. She ended the call. "My boss. The card club is opening this weekend. He wants me there."

"Wow, the government is really pushing to get everything moving again," Robbie said.

Morgan laughed. "My boss was chomping at the bit to re-open. There's money to be made. You know people tend to gamble more when things get nuts, right?"

Robbie laughed. "Reminds me of what one of my friends told me," he said. "About Valley Forge."

"One of those friends?" She nodded to the living room.

"No, one of my fellow bloggers. He lives in Valley Forge, in a house built in 1730. Cool place. I got to visit there once. Some of Washington's officers actually lived there during the Revolutionary War."

"Wow," Morgan said. "What does that have to do with gambling?"

"General Washington got alarmed because his troops were gambling too much. They used dice. Washington confiscated all of the dice to stop it."

"Wow, never heard that story," Morgan said.

"It gets better," Robbie said. "The soldiers started carving their musket balls into dice. There were so many sets of homemade dice in the dirt out there that just about everybody who lives there has found some. My friend had two sets. Found them in his garden while he was planting flowers."

"You're kidding," Morgan said.

"Human nature," Robbie said. "People find ways to relieve pressure in times like these. Gambling is one way."

"I know what another way is," Morgan said. She looked at him with a sly smile.

Robbie moved in and kissed her.

***

Sam, Connie, Officer Ryan, and Officer Patrick stood by the mobile artillery piece behind the clubhouse, looking it over and chatting. Clem hurried out to them.

"Hey, guys, let's go in the clubhouse," Clem said. "Things just went nuts."

He turned and trotted back to the clubhouse. Connie looked at Sam, worry in her eyes.

"What the hell happened now?" Ryan asked.

"C'mon," Sam said. They rushed into the clubhouse.

"Dammit, is that New York Harbor?" Patrick asked, looking at the TV screen.

"Yeah," Clem said. "Somebody floated a nuke in there. They just announced that a bomb went off in Puget Sound too."

"Son of a bitch," Ryan said.

Connie trembled and started to cry, Sam pulling her close.

"This changes everything," Clem said.

"Yeah it does," Sam said, his brow furrowed, anger in his eyes. "They've signed their own death warrants now."

"Look, one went off in a Russian harbor too," Clem said, pointing to the text streaming along the bottom of the screen.

"Hell, look at it now," Ryan said. "They hit Charleston Harbor too."

Ryan's lapel radio scratched. "Ryan, you there?"

"Excuse me a moment," he said. "Patrick, c'mon. Outside."

The two officers went through the door. Connie, Clem, and Sam looked at each other. John and Sarah rushed in.

"You see what happened?" Sarah asked, tears streaming down her face.

"Yeah," Sam said. "We're under attack."

"Big time," John said.

"You don't think it's the Russians, do you?" Sarah asked.

"No, they got hit too," Clem said.

"This was Islamists and somebody else, I suspect," Sam said. "Things are gonna get crazy now."

Ryan and Patrick came back in.

"We gotta go," Ryan said. "The brass is calling everybody in."

"Because of this?" John asked.

"No, because our idiot Governor and the President invited somebody else into the party," Patrick said.

"Who?" Sam asked.

"The frigging UN," Ryan said. "Idiots. The Administration is targeting *domestic terrorism*."

Clem laughed. "Oh, please. The enemy is coming over the Mexican border and from the coast."

"At least they didn't call it workplace violence," John said.

Sam and Clem chuckled. Ryan and Patrick looked deadly serious.

"We need you to let us out," Ryan said. "Lock up after we leave. Don't let the UN come in here. If I were you I'd take that mobile artillery out there and point it down the damn access road."

"You sound pissed," Clem said.

"You're damn straight I'm pissed," Ryan said. "In my book this is treason."

"Yeah, that's what I'd call it," Sam said. "You can't bring in foreign soldiers to control our population."

Clem laughed. "Yeah, only *we* can do that."

Patrick shook his head. "You know, he's got a point, Ryan. Now we're gonna find out how it feels."

"Don't get me wrong, boys," Clem said. "I'll fight these Euro-trash idiots to the death."

"How do you know they're from Europe?" Ryan asked.

"Because this is exactly the kind of crap I'd expect from Brussels," Clem said. "Remember when half the countries left the EU about ten years ago? The Globalists haven't given up even after that rebuke, if you've noticed."

"I noticed," John said.

"Okay, I'll go get the gate opened for you," Sam said.

"I'm going with you," Connie said. "I don't want you out of my sight right now."

"No problem, sweetie," Sam said. They walked out the door with Ryan and Patrick.

"What do the UN vehicles look like?" Connie asked.

"White and blue," Ryan said. "Usually marked with a big *UN* on the sides and back."

"What about Europe?" Sam asked. "I'd think they would be in more trouble than we are. Look at their population. They let in all those radicals before the partial collapse of the EU, remember? As far as I know, most of them are still there."

"Britain deported a lot of them. So did France and the Netherlands after they left the EU," Ryan said. "Still a big problem, though."

"You've been following this, obviously," Connie said.

"Yeah," Ryan said. "See you guys at the gate."

Ryan and Patrick got back into their cruiser. Connie and Sam got into the Jeep. They drove down to the gate.

"You folks take care, and keep your eyes open," Ryan said. "Remember what I said – about the National Guard and the UN."

"Which is it more likely to be?" Connie asked.

"I have no idea," Ryan said. "The brass isn't accepting the authority of the UN. We've been told to arrest any UN personnel trying to push American citizens around. The Governor might step in and remove our leadership, though. If they do that, I'm done. I'm joining the resistance."

"Yeah, me too," Patrick said.

"You could always come here and join us," Sam said.

"I'll keep it in mind," Ryan said. "You guys have me impressed." He watched as Sam opened the gate. Then he and Patrick got back in their cruiser and drove away. Sam closed the gate, locked it, and reset the alarm.

"My God," Connie said. "What the hell is going on?"

"A lot more than the authorities want us to know," Sam said. "Somebody is going to mess with us over that pass. I can feel it coming."

"You really going to point that artillery piece down the road?"

Sam chuckled as they got back into the Jeep.

"No, I think that would be a bad idea," he said.

"Why?"

"First off, we have the Tigr, and that ought to be enough. Secondly, that artillery could bring down the side of the mountain over our little road. If that happens, we won't be able to drive out of here. Be different if we had a bulldozer, but we don't."

"Oh," Connie said. "So what do we do?"

"Wait, watch, and keep a cool head," Sam said. "At least we've taken care of the immediate Islamist problem."

"Wonder who's worse?" Connie asked. "The Islamists or the UN?"

"That's the real question," Sam said, as he started the Jeep and k-turned, heading back to the RV Park.

17

World at War

Seth rushed down to Emma as the others helped Ji-Ho bring the guns off the rooftop deck.

"The police are going to come get us," Emma said.

"I wouldn't worry about it," Seth said. "We just sank five boatloads of invaders. Then the navy came along and sank the main boat. I don't think we're in trouble. If anything, they'll thank us."

Emma looked at him, still trembling. "Hold me, dummy."

Seth pulled her close, hugging her as she sobbed against his chest.

Kaylee and Matt came inside. "You okay, Emma?" she asked.

"I'm okay," she said. "I don't like this."

"None of us like this," Matt said.

Ji-Ho walked in with Angel and Trevor.

"Anything else happen?" Seth asked.

"No," Ji-Ho said. "I call police chief and tell. He fine. We fine."

"So what now?" Emma asked.

"Nothing," Trevor said. "We just did a good thing. Don't worry about it."

"Let's watch the news for a while," Matt said. "Maybe they'll say something."

Ji-Ho picked up the remote and clicked on the TV. "Hungry?"

"Kaylee and I will whip something up," Emma said. "We found what we needed."

"Ah, very good," Ji-Ho said. "Many thanks."

"Thank you for giving us a place to stay," Matt said.

"Yes, thanks," Trevor said. The others nodded in agreement.

"Hey, look at the screen!" Jamie said.

"What is that?" Trevor asked. "Is that New York Harbor?"

"Oh no," Kaylee said, staring wide-eyed at the screen. "What happened?"

Everybody sat, watching silently as the screen showed video of the devastation.

"Look at the banner at the bottom of the screen," Emma said. "Nuclear attacks in New York and Seattle."

"Oh no," Ji-Ho said. "No no no."

"What if they do that here?" Emma asked, clutching Seth.

"Could they?" Kaylee asked.

"Wonder what the guys in those boats were doing?" Trevor asked.

"Getting ready for an attack like this, perhaps," Angel said. "Dammit."

"Nothing blew up out there," Emma said.

"Nuclear bombs have to be detonated," Jamie said. "They won't go off in an explosion."

"He right," Ji-Ho said. "This very bad. Hope wife okay in Korea. I worried."

"Why would Korea be a target?" Kaylee asked.

"North Korea have bombs," Ji-Ho said, looking at her in fear. "Maybe they provide. Things get hot fast."

"She's not next to the border, though, right?" Kaylee asked.

"No, she south, but maybe not enough," Ji-Ho said. "Local news commentator come on. I turn up."

"The attacks in New York, Puget Sound, Vladivostok, and Charleston Harbor have local authorities on alert. All harbors and

marinas in the area are on lockdown, and all vessels large and small are being searched at this hour."

"They wouldn't have to hit a harbor in this area," Trevor said. "They could float something into Santa Monica Bay and blow it there. The wind would drive the radiation right into the major population centers."

"Lovely thought," Jamie said. Seth shot both of them a glare as Emma trembled against him.

They watched the news silently for a while, nobody knowing what to say. Jamie finally got up and walked to the windows, looking out over the blue Pacific. "There's a lot of patrol boats out there now," he said. "Big coast guard cutters. They probably got the same idea Trevor did."

Angel, Matt, and Ji-Ho all went to the windows and looked.

"Wow, big operation," Ji-Ho said. "Good. They keep enemy boats away. We probably safe."

"Should we go?" Emma asked.

"Go where?" Seth asked.

"I don't know. Inland. Maybe your grandparent's cabin."

"You won't make it," Trevor said. "We'll be under martial law in the next few hours. They're already closing down roads. You'd never make it past all the checkpoints."

"This is still America," Seth said.

"Trevor right," Ji-Ho said. "Police chief tell me. City put in grids with checkpoints. Residents only, unless have job in area. Will be very tight."

"With all the cross streets around here, their controls are gonna leak," Jamie said. "There will be ways around the checkpoints."

"Maybe, but don't get caught in wrong area without papers," Ji-Ho said. "Police or National Guard arrest."

"You sound like you've lived this before," Angel said.

"Most of earth not free like America," Ji-Ho said. "Even South Korea. Government push people around during crisis. Everybody is suspect. Very bad. Wish I went with wife."

"Why didn't you?" Kaylee asked.

"Business," he said. "Can't leave. Might not be able to come back if leave now."

"You're probably right there," Trevor said.

"Can we go in the bedroom?" Emma asked. "I just want to curl up in a ball next to you and sleep."

"Don't you feel safer out here with everybody else?" Seth asked.

"No," she said. "I want you to hold me. I'll make it worth your while."

Seth shook his head. "I'll cuddle with you. You don't have to bribe me. C'mon."

They left the room.

"She's really shook up," Kaylee said.

"Of course she is," Matt said. "She's a total control freak. This situation is very *out-of-control*."

"Be nice," Kaylee said.

"Oh, come on, sweetie," he said. "I'm not being mean. It's how she is. You know that."

"I know, but you don't have to say it that way," Kaylee said. "Guess I'm cooking dinner by myself."

"I'll help you," Matt said, getting up and holding his hand out to her. She took it and got up. When they got into the kitchen she hugged him.

"I'm pretty upset too, you know," she said. "Can you hold me for a minute?"

"Of course," Matt said, holding her tight.

"No!" Ji-Ho shouted from the living room.

Kaylee's eyes opened wide, and she looked up at Matt. They rushed back into the living room.

"What happened?" Kaylee asked. Ji-Ho had tears running down his cheeks.

"Russia just told China to move their forces away from the border of North Korea or risk losing them," Trevor said. "The nuclear devices *did* come from there."

"Oh no," Kaylee said, rushing over to hug Ji-Ho.

"If she's in the south she'll probably be okay," Matt said.

"North Korean leadership nuts," Ji-Ho said. "They might fire all they have at South Korea."

"They might fire some of it towards Japan, Russia, and the US," Jamie said. "Look at the screen."

There was a graphic showing a world map, with circles around North Korea for each type of missile they have.

"See, their best missile could hit the west coast of the US," Jamie said.

Trevor shook his head. "Japan and South Korea have a big reason to worry," he said. "Remember that there's been no successful tests of the longest-range North Korean missiles. Most of the time they blow up shortly after takeoff."

"I think a lot of their failures have happened because we've shot down their missiles," Jamie said. "They should've made more progress in the last ten years."

"He right," Ji-Ho said. "Small comfort for me, but I wouldn't worry about North Korea hitting US. Even Japan is big job for them."

"All they have to do is get lucky a few times," Angel said. "This sucks."

"I go try to call wife," Ji-Ho said, leaving the room.

"He's so worried," Kaylee said. "Me too."

***

Robbie was shutting down his laptop, Morgan next to him. "Almost dark," he said.

"Yeah, and no gunfire in the distance," Morgan said. "That's a good thing, hopefully."

"Hopefully," Robbie said, touching her shoulder. She smiled at him and put her hand on his.

They went into the living room and sat down with the others in front of the TV.

"Anything new going on?" Morgan asked.

"Evacuations," Gil said. "They're moving people away from San Pedro and Long Beach."

"The harbors," Robbie said.

"Uh oh," Morgan said. "They find something?"

"Not yet," Gil said, "but they nabbed a pleasure boat in Baltimore's inner harbor just before the Islamists were going to set off a nuke."

"That's really close to DC," Morgan said.

"Sure is," Justin said.

"Steve and Colleen are still downstairs?" Robbie asked.

"Yeah, but they're being quiet this time," Gil said.

"Maybe they're just being together," Morgan said. "Colleen was really scared. Sometimes we just like to be held, you know."

"Yeah, maybe," Justin said. "Wish I had a girlfriend. A real one, that is."

"The plastic blow-up one getting old?" Gil asked.

Robbie laughed. "Ouch."

Justin snickered. "Shut up. Everybody doesn't have to know."

"You guys are crazy," Morgan said.

"I do have a girlfriend, by the way," Justin said to Morgan, "but we've been drifting apart. She left town with her parents. Hadn't seen her for a few weeks before that, so I'm guessing it's *really* over now."

"Why don't you make a move on Steve's sister?" Gil asked. "We all know you like her."

"She's got a boyfriend, remember?" Justin said.

"Steve told me that was on the rocks," Gil said. "You ought to ask him about it. Katie's *fine*, and I've seen her check you out before."

"We'll see," Justin said.

"Pussy," Gil said. "You won't do anything."

"That doesn't make him a pussy," Robbie said. "Think about it. If it doesn't go well, he runs the risk of losing his friendship with Steve."

"Good point," Morgan said. "Seen that happen before."

"Thanks for that vote of confidence," Justin said.

"I still say he's a pussy," Gil said.

Robbie's phone rang. He looked at the number. "It's my mom. Good. Tried to get her a couple times earlier. No dice." He put the phone to his ear.

"Robbie?"

"Mom, you got through. I've been trying to call you for a while now. It's nearly impossible to get a call to connect from here."

"Well, it's probably like when we have an earthquake," she said. "You know how they tell you to call a relative out of state?"

"You guys *are* out of state," Robbie said. "Everything's screwed up."

"You've been watching the news, right?"

"Yes, all of the nuke attacks. Geez," Robbie said.

"Are they saying anything about LA Harbor?"

"Yes, they've been moving people out of the areas right around LA and Long Beach harbors."

"Do you think you're all right where you are?"

"I think so. We're pretty far away from the big harbors. The closest thing to us is Marina Del Rey, and there aren't any large ships in there."

"Good," his mom said.

"Oh crap," Robbie said. "Big flash to the north…"

There was static on the line, and it disconnected.

"What the hell was that?" cried Morgan, rushing next to Robbie.

"I'll bet that was a nuke," Gil said.

"Marina Del Rey?" Justin asked, terror in his eyes.

"No way," Robbie said. "We would have felt it. We'd probably be dead already."

The door downstairs opened, Steve and Colleen running up the stairs.

"What was that?" Steve asked. "It lit up the room."

Colleen clutched Steve, trembling.

Gil pointed to the screen. "Special bulletin on TV."

"We have received a statement from the White House that retaliation has started, and will be working its way from the closest perpetrators outward. Venezuela has just been rocked by nuclear attacks in all of its ports and all of its major population centers."

"Whoa," Robbie said.

"Steve," Colleen said, turning against him and sobbing.

"Look at the TV now," Morgan said. "They're about to tell us what happened here, I'll bet."

"This just in. A small device was detonated in Southern California, in Ventura Harbor. This harbor was not considered a threat. Now all of the municipalities with small harbors are on alert, and all boats are being searched."

"This is horrible," Steve said.

"The Cities of Ventura and Oxnard have sustained large loss of life and catastrophic damage. The prevailing wind is to the east, which will cause problems for the rich agricultural area that lies in that direction. Authorities have said they will require evacuation of people as far east as Simi Valley due to the fallout danger. There are also plans to evacuate the nearby communities of Thousand Oaks and Agoura. At this time, it appears that the nearest big population areas up and down the coast will survive and not need evacuation. These communities include Santa Barbara to the north and the cities along Santa Monica Bay to the south."

"Oh, geez," Robbie said. "All those people. My God."

"They're gonna check the sporting marinas around here now," Gil said. "King Harbor in Redondo, and Marina Del Rey."

"Yeah," Justin said. "Probably down south too. Huntington, Cabrillo, Newport, and the others."

"What's your mom gonna think?" Morgan asked.

"She's probably out of her mind right now," Robbie said. He tried to call her. "Still can't call out of the area. Hopefully she saw the news report that it was Ventura."

"What should we do?" Colleen asked.

"Not much we can do," Steve said. "It's far away. It won't affect us directly."

"Look, something else is happening," Gil said, nodding to the TV.

"More?" Colleen asked. She looked shell shocked.

"In other news," the announcer continued, *"Russia has started using the same strategy in their country to take out the radical Islamists, which is to take out the closest bases first, and then expand outward. They have chosen not to use nuclear weapons near their country. They are using a scorched earth eradication in areas of their country that are linked to the device in Vladivostok. At the current hour, they have leveled all mosques in Chechnya, and are searching house to house for Islamist leaders in that province. The UN and Amnesty International are already protesting the actions."*

Gil laughed. "Yeah, let them protest, but stay the hell out of the way."

Justin glanced at him.

"What?" Gil asked.

"Nothing," Justin said. "I actually agree with you this time."

"Glory be," Robbie said.

"This isn't something to joke about," Colleen said.

"I'm not," Robbie said. "Really."

"Breaking news," the announcer said. *"A device has been located in the San Francisco Bay area, on a large private yacht. There is a manhunt going on right now to find the perpetrators. The owners of the yacht were found below deck. All of them had been murdered."*

"Thank God they found that," Justin said. "You know how dense the population is up there?"

"Yeah, seriously," Gil said. "Geez, what a frigging night."

"I just want it to be over," Colleen said.

"The White House has announced a press conference for 10:00 PM EST tonight," the announcer said. *"And it is expected that the Russian president will join him for part of the briefing."*

"Oh, great," Gil said.

"We need to stick together now," Justin said. "No BS."

"Okay, you got me there," Gil said. "I'm willing to listen, even if I can't stand the guy."

"Can we go back downstairs?" Colleen asked.

"The President is gonna be on pretty soon. Why don't we stay up here until then?"

"Okay," Colleen said.

"Thanks," Steve said, putting his arms around her.

"I need a beer," Robbie said. "Anybody else?"

"Yeah, I'll take one," Gil said.

"Me too," Justin said.

Steve shook his head no.

"Honey?" Robbie asked, looking at Morgan.

"Honey?" She giggled.

"Sorry," he said. "Too soon?"

Morgan smiled. "No. I'll go with you and help."

She got up and the two of them went into the kitchen. As they were getting beer out of the fridge, Robbie's phone rang.

"Hey, Robbie, your phone is ringing," Justin shouted.

"Coming," Robbie said. He and Morgan returned with bottles. Robbie set two bottles on the coffee table and grabbed his phone.

"Mom," Robbie said.

"Yes, honey, it's your father and me. I've got you on speaker."

"I tried to call you back, but still can't connect from here," Robbie said. "You heard about what happened in Ventura?"

"Yes, son," his mom said.

"We were afraid it happened in Del Rey," his dad said.

"We'd be toast if that happened. They should have crews looking through the boats in Redondo Harbor and Marina Del Rey by now. Also down south in all of the pleasure boat harbors. You heard about the yacht up in Frisco, right?"

"Yes, we've had the news on the radio," mom said. "We're going to the clubhouse in a few minutes. They have a couple of big screens with CNN and Fox News on over there."

"And a bunch of food too," his dad added. "How are your supplies holding up there?"

"We're in good shape, dad."

"Hey, got a bottle opener?" Gil asked.

Robbie nodded yes, then got up and walked into the kitchen while he was still talking. He heard gasps from the living room, so he rushed out with the bottle opener, eyes getting wide when he saw the screen.

"Wow!" Robbie exclaimed. "A nuke just went off in Paris. They just put pictures up."

"Oh no, Paris too?" his mom asked. Robbie could hear her crying. "When is this going to stop?"

"It just got announced on the radio," his dad said. "Listen."

"Robbie, we gotta go," his mom said. "Take care of yourself. Love you."

"Love you too, mom, and you too dad," Robbie said.

"Love you, son," his dad said. "Be careful." Robbie set down his phone, wiping the tears off his cheek. Morgan rushed over and held him as the others watched Paris burning.

"The world will never be the same," Justin said.

"I know," Gil said, wiping his eyes. "Paris. My God. It's all gone."

"The device was probably in a boat on the Seine river," the announcer said. *"This is the worst attack yet. It happened in a very densely populated area. This one is going to have a death toll in the millions."*

"Millions?" Colleen asked, eyes red from crying. "I can't take this anymore, Steve. Can't we go downstairs?"

"Okay," Steve said, petting her head as he looked at her with tenderness. They walked downstairs as the others continued to stare at the screen in disbelief.

The commentators came back on the screen. It was a young woman and an older man. They both looked exhausted.

"We have received a video from an Islamist leader in Iraq," said the male commentator. *"It arrived on YouTube less than half an hour ago."*

"We bring it to you now, uncut," the woman said.

The video displayed on the screen. There was an old man in a white robe, with a long beard and a round hat. He was sitting on a rug. On either side of him stood younger men with long beards, dressed in black, holding automatic weapons. Behind them was the logo of the terror organization that had recently taken over a large chunk of both Syria and Iraq.

The old man started to speak, his lips moving with no sound coming out. Then an English translator spoke.

"By the grace of Allah, I am here to announce a new Caliphate. We have taken the battle to the Infidel in every corner of the western world, and we have just begun. Truly all praise belongs to Allah. We and our partners have placed agents in every corner of your free

societies, and will use your own laws to bring you under the control of Allah and Muhammad (peace and blessings be upon him) His slave and Messenger. I have been declared the new Caliph of the global Islamic State."

"What a jerk," Gil said. "We're gonna fry your ass."

The Caliph continued.

"The peoples of the world will agree that they will submit to Allah, or accept dhimmi status."

"What's dhimmi status?" asked Morgan.

"The attacks will not stop, as you are not yet convinced that you cannot defeat Allah and his armies…Allah willing, and nothing is too great for Allah."

The video ended abruptly.

"Looks like that was censored," Justin said.

"What's dhimmi status?" asked Morgan again.

"Sorry," Robbie said. "It's a kind of second-class citizenship that Muslim countries impose on non-believers – as long as they are Christians or Jews."

"Yeah, *people of the book,*" Justin said.

"What do you mean by second-class citizenship?" Morgan asked.

"You have to pay a tax for being a non-believer, and there are a bunch of restrictions put on you."

"Yeah," Justin said. "They treat non-believers the way certain minorities used to be treated in certain parts of this country."

"Oh, like Jim Crow laws?" Morgan asked.

"Yeah, only worse," Robbie said.

"Geez," Morgan said. "Guess I should read up on all this."

"I can help you there," Robbie said. "Spent a lot of time on that lately."

"Look, the President is coming on," Justin said.

"We now take you to the White House," the woman commentator said.

The screen displayed a briefing room with an empty podium. The presidential seal was on the front of it, and there were flags on either side.

"That's a secure location," Gil said. "Not the White House."

"I would *hope* they have him at a secure location," Justin said.

"Seriously," Morgan said.

"Here comes the President," Robbie said.

The screen showed him walking up to the podium. He had a somber look on his face.

"Good evening, ladies and gentlemen. I won't recount what has happened over the last twenty-four hours, as I'm sure all of you have been following the news. The United States, the EU, and the Russian Federation are cooperating on a level not seen since the Second World War, to settle this matter and bring the guilty parties to justice. And make no mistake, our response will not be a restrained series of police actions. These attacks are acts of war, and will be treated as such. We will use our most terrible weapons, and fight as if our very survival is at stake, because it is."

"Good," Gil said. "Hope he means it."

"Shut up," Justin said. Gil shot him a sidelong grin. Morgan smirked and shook her head.

"A few words about moderate Muslims. There is no cause and no excuse to punish our moderate Muslim citizens due to the actions of these radicals. Remember that moderate Muslims living in our cities have been killed in these attacks, right alongside people of every other faith. That being said, the United States is not going to have the resources to protect all of you at all times from angry citizens. I suggest that you keep a low profile while we concern ourselves with winning this war."

"Finally, a few words about martial law. We have put that in place only in areas that are under attack, and we will not leave it in place for long. I know there are many out there who are concerned about

the guarantees of liberty which reside in our Bill of Rights. This Administration takes those guarantees very seriously. martial law will only be declared when we need it to fight the enemy. Rumors of an extension of martial law to all areas of the United States are false. We have no reason to do that. We will not do that. I hope that puts these fears to rest. That is all for now, and sorry, but I won't take any questions at this time." He left the podium and walked off to the right.

"Holy shit," Robbie said.

"What?" Justin asked.

"He just told Muslims that they'd better not try to use our laws against us," Robbie said.

"You think that's what he was saying?" Justin asked.

"Yep," Robbie said.

"Oh no," Morgan said, pointing to the screen. "That's London."

"No," Justin said as he watched fire and people running around on the video.

The commentator came back on the screen.

"That amazing footage was taken in Westminster. About an hour ago, the British Secret Service foiled a nuclear attack on the city. It was on another pleasure craft, on the Thames River. The device was disarmed and all suspects were apprehended. According to BBC they were of Pakistani and Syrian nationality."

"Good," Morgan said. "Glad they stopped them.

The announcer continued.

"As you can see, we have fires burning in the background. At the time that the news about the foiled nuclear attack was released, Islamic demonstrators were still camped outside Westminster Abbey. Men flooded out of the nearby pubs, beat most of the demonstrators to death, and burned their tents, signs, and other items. London police looked on, but took no action."

"That's going to shut down operations at the radical mosques in London," Gil said.

"You think what happened there is good?" Justin asked.

"Yeah, as a matter of fact," Gil said.

"Hey, quiet, there's something else happening," Robbie said.

The screen now went to another special bulletin. The commentators were back on, looking at papers on their desk. They both looked really tired.

"Ladies and Gentlemen, we have two more major stories to report. First, the United States Government has announced that it is moving into Mexico to take control of that country, in lieu of an official Mexican government. The agents from Venezuela who had attempted to take over have fled that country after Mexican nationals stormed the palace. The United States is coming in at the request of what is left of the Mexican government. They will not answer questions about the length of the occupation or plans for the future."

"Wow," Gil said. "That'll piss some people off."

"The second story comes out of North and South Korea. United States and South Korean troops are evacuating from the border next to the de-militarized zone, at the same time that the Chinese are pulling their troops away from the northern border of North Korea. It is widely expected that a major attack is imminent, and sources say that North Korea is getting ready to fire their ICBMs in desperation. South Korea and Japan are trying to protect their people as best they can, and missile defense units are at the ready. Although untested, North Korean ICBMs do have the capability to hit the western United States as well as the Russian Federation and other Asian countries."

Morgan shook with fear and grabbed Robbie's arm. He pulled her close, her head against his chest. "Don't worry, honey," he murmured as he stroked her hair. *Can I protect her?* His righteous indignation blasted to the surface, his free hand balling into a fist. *Damn right I can.*

To be continued in Bug Out! California Book 2

Cast Of Characters

Note: some of these characters are not in the first book. They will show up later in the story.

Dulzura RV Park Group – Mostly retired people, but mixed. Full-timers.

John – Older man, drinking problem, but fighting it. Brave and strong.

Sarah – John's wife. Doesn't his like drinking, but loyal anyway. Good heart.

Clem – Old widower. Shrewd with sense of humor, and technically savvy.

Sid – Indian, capable, good man in fight, loyal, cunning.

Yvonne – Sid's wife. Resourceful and brave. Younger than him by ten years

Harry – Older man, heavy, doesn't move well, good negotiator and strategist.

Nancy – Harry's wife, retired school teacher. Smart but has problems with stress.

Sam – Owner of RV Park. Middle aged, strong, wily, cautious. Former Navy Seal with some PTSD issues, which he has mostly under control. Good in a fight, knows modern military tactics and weapons systems.

Connie – Wife of Sam. Thinks one step ahead. Keeps park running. Deeply in love with Sam.

CHP Officer Ryan – Older officer. Brave, sense of humor, borderline redneck, good in fight, but has temper.

CHP Officer Patrick – Just past rookie status. Extremely good with guns. A little green. A little hapless. Good in fight. Brave to a fault.

Jack, aka One Eye – Barona Indian, friend of Sid's who helps at the battle of Fernbrook.

Hank – police officer in the town of Julian. Older man, gray hair, feisty. Joins group after they destroy the enemy checkpoint in his town. Works with Jason.

Jason – police officer in town of Julian. Younger, fast with a gun, smart as a whip. Aggressive. Joins group after they destroy the enemy checkpoint in his town. Works with Hank.

Kaitlyn aka Still Pool – young woman in Barona Tribe. Curvy, pretty face, strong personality. Goes after what she wants, loyal and passionate, smart.

Megan aka Sage Flower – young woman in Barona Tribe. Tiny, delicate beauty, feisty, loud, aggressive, brave, smart. Wicked sense of humor.

Zac aka Sandy Creek - young Indian warrior. Brave and handsome, cunning.

James aka Crossbow – young Indian warrior, expert with weapons, especially crossbows. Brave, funny sense of humor, loved by the tribe.

Ryan aka Touchdown – young Indian warrior, brave, fast, CIF MVP in High School, great in a fight.

Tyler aka Quiet Fox – young Indian Warrior, smart, thinks a couple levels deep, quiet, reserved, observes and thinks before acting, usually makes right choice. Future Chief.

Nurse Grace – Emergency room nurse, taking care of Sam and Connie at the hospital in La Quinta. Pretty middle-aged woman, tough as nails and smart as a whip.

Kenny – warrior with the Barona Tribe.

Bradley – warrior with the Barona Tribe.

Silver Wolf – overall chief of the Barona Tribe. Older man, medium build, looks younger than his years. Total tech nut, very talented and inventive.

Kerry aka Yellow Bird – young warrior. Fast, too emotional. Unpredictable.

Shane aka Red Snake – warrior, a little older, family man but also great fighter.

Will aka Swimming Bear – warrior, early thirties, negotiator, helps Silver Wolf with technology.

Mia – wife of Tyler. Strong, beautiful, smart. Delicate features, hair-trigger emotions.

Riley – wife of Ryan. Very small, below five feet tall. Beautiful face. Has Ryan wrapped around her finger.

Abby – wife of James – heavy set larger woman with an infectious smile and a gentle, kind way about her. Beautiful face.

Redondo Condo group – Thirty-something

Robbie – Thirty-something son of Frank and Jane from original series. Brave, thoughtful, writer, shy, cynical

Morgan – neighbor of Robbie, love interest. Strong, more outgoing and aggressive than Robbie, pretty, transplant from Utah, good with guns.

Gil – Robbie's best friend from High School. Hispanic. Good with guns, brave, sense of humor, cautious, protective.

Steve – Robbie's friend from college. Smart but not serious, surfer, scrappy, good in fight

Justin – Robbie's friend from high school and college. Sparks with others, temper, suspicious nature but good heart

Killer – Pit Bull – from Justin's family. Strong, protective, dangerous to evil-doers.

Colleen – girlfriend of Steve. Beautiful redhead. Flighty, aggressive, but loyal and loving.

Katie – Steve's sister. Strong, rebellious, great in a fight, beautiful. Justin adores her. She brings out his courage.

Cody – neighbor who lives across the street from Frank and Jane's Condo. Friends with them. Tough reserve police officer and early resistance fighter. Large muscular man in his early thirties with a military style haircut, light brown hair, and a goatee.

Sparky – Morgan's boss at the card club. Big, dangerous man with a shady past but a good heart. Protects his employees to a fault. Has underworld connections. Not a good person to mess with.

Ivan the Butcher – mob boss. Most people assume he's from Russia, but he's actually an American who built his organization in Russia and Europe, before being hounded back home by the EU authorities. Dangerous and unpredictable, but a strategic thinker. Childhood friend of Sparky.

Jules – right hand man of Ivan the Butcher. Belgian national, good in a fight, a little crazy but very calculating.

Tex – Friend of Sparky and Jules. Crazy with wicked sense of humor, great in a fight, brave to a fault.

Ted – Robbie's boss at the restaurant. Former Navy Seal, tricked into joining the battle by Sparky. Old friends with Ivan the Butcher.

Stacey – cook in Ted's restaurant, acquaintance of Robbie's. Heavy-set large man, good in a fight, not the brightest but loyal and brave to a fault.

Jordan – black man, former Army Ranger. Near genius tactical expert. Brave and cunning, trusts nobody until he's sure, then as loyal as the day is long. Wicked sense of humor.

Dana – beautiful girl who was kidnapped by the UN to use as a sex slave. Rescued by Jules's team after the battle at Torrance Civic Center.

Karen – beautiful redhead, daughter of Gil's boss. Captured and held at the Torrance Police Station with the other girls. Not sure where she fits in the group.

Tisha – wild young woman, former captive. Small, tattooed and pierced, fiery, hard to handle, brave and loyal but prickly. Passionate.

Alexis - a brunette with a hauntingly beautiful face and a thin build. Tough and loyal but with a sadness in her that she battles constantly. Valuable member of the team.

Brooke - tall, dark haired beauty with a strong build and a defensive demeanor. Lesbian. Protective of her woman. Fierce, loyal fighter. Touchy but with a good heart. Smart.

Audrey – Doctor. Lesbian, close to Brooke. A small waif with ginger hair and freckles.

Lily – a small blonde, willowy, with a delicate face. Has emotional issues. Bipolar. Suicidal. Barely survived captivity.

Shelly – short, perky blonde with a beautiful face and a way with organization. Valuable member of the team.

Ashley - Curly-haired brunette with a dancer's body and grace, with a quiet demeanor. Not sure she's up to the fight, but feels it's her duty. Likes Jordan, because they both have the theater bug.

Brianna - a young-looking girl with an innocent face and curly light brown hair. Not very confident. Frightened by the war. Stacey is pursuing her, and she's okay with it, but not passionate.

Haley - an ice blond with a curvy figure and a lot of self-confidence. Good fighter.

Allison - a redhead of medium build. She has a country look to her, innocent but with a touch of mischief. Expert hunter and backpacker, champion level shooter. Ready for anything. Will become a principle in the group over time.

South Torrance Group – Ages from 19 to 24. Well-to-do parents. Some recently on their own, some live with parents. Gun hobbyists. Immature but with enthusiasm.

Seth – defacto leader of group due to calm, easy going nature mixed with charisma. Gets along with everybody in group. Slightly more mature than the others. Has serious girlfriend, centers his life around her, in love.

Emma – Seth's girlfriend. Beautiful, was popular in high school, aggressive, controlling, but nice, loyal. Needs Seth when she gets scared or upset. Doesn't like Matt or Trevor much. Feeling is mutual. Likes Angel.

Trevor – talented, brilliant, great with guns, nutty, good sense of humor. Aggressive with temper. Likes to argue. Younger than the others by a year. Came into group as Seth's friend, closest to him.

Angel – cynical sense of humor, honest and trustworthy. Hispanic. Lives with family, but inching out. Good in fight. Seth's best friend. Pivotal member of group, head for business and practicality. Slightly more mature than the others.

Matt – Angel's oldest friend. Funny, problems with drinking, emotional, secondary leader who sparks with Seth sometimes, but they are close in ways the others aren't. Good in fight, image is important to him, womanizer. Has serious girlfriend but cheats on her.

Kaylee – Matt's girlfriend. Nice, talented, good friend of Emma, clueless about Matt's infidelity, doesn't like him drinking, getting tired of his childish behavior. Beautiful in an exotic way, Korean.

Ji-Ho – Kaylee's rich uncle, lives in compound on north-west side of Palos Verdes, overlooking ocean. Brave and smart, loyal, understands what it's like when government gets too much control. Can relate well to younger people, even though his English isn't great.

Gus – combat tactics trainer, met group at gun range. Great organizer and leader. Serious. Destined for greatness if he lives long enough.

Government/Authorities

Governor Sable – fourth-term governor of California. Old-style liberal – coming to the conclusion that there really is something wrong with the Administration. Knows how to do the right thing, and usually does after fits and starts. Watch out when he gets angry.

Jennifer – Sable's black secretary. They were lovers years ago, now friends, but Nancy keeps her distance because Sable still loves her. Competent and smart – Sable's underground advisor.

Saladin – evil Islamic leader, trying to move the US towards martial law with terror attacks. Acting in collusion with the President and others. Kills without mercy or regard for innocent bystanders. Pretends to be pious, but only uses his religion to gain power. Human trash.

Commissioner Frawley – head of CHP for California. Currently in prison after going against the Governor and the Administration. Strong character, brave, will make difference.

Deputy Commissioner Katz – second in command at CHP – also in prison. Hates jihadists. Dangerous man to his enemies. Near-genius intelligence.

Assistant Commissioner Cooley – third in command at CHP, in prison with other two commissioners. Black man. Brave, strong, emotional, smart. Always has your back. Wicked sense of humor.

Chief Smith – turncoat chief of CHP – helped capture the commissioners. No stomach for violence. A coward, only in his

{ 229 }

position because he's related to Sable. Follows whoever he's most scared of at any given time. Trusts nobody, in it for himself.

President Simpson – ineffective, corrupt leader of the United States. In league with the enemy.

Attorney General Blake – Simpson's right-hand man. Corrupt and evil.

ABOUT THE AUTHOR

Robert G Boren is a writer from the South Bay section of Southern California. He writes Short Stories, Novels, and Serialized Fiction.

Made in the USA
Coppell, TX
03 December 2019